THE KENDRICK GIRLS

Christmas Eve, 1905 ... After the murder, many were doubtful that a young woman like Barbara Kendrick could have committed such an act. Although it pleased the romantics to think that she had killed him out of jealousy, the truth was stranger than that and far less simple. Even those who knew her best had no conception of what had really happened. In the end, by her own actions, she wove for herself a net of misfortune, for she did indeed have a heavy debt to pay, but not quite in the way that everyone supposed ...

THE KENDRICK GIRLS

by

Elizabeth Ann Hill

Magna Large Print Books
Long Preston, North Yorkshire,
England.

British Library Cataloguing in Publication Data.

Hill, Elizabeth Ann
  The Kendrick girls.

  A catalogue record for this book is
  available from the British Library

  ISBN 0-7505-1297-0

First published in Great Britain by Severn House Publishers
Ltd., 1997

Copyright © 1981, 1997 by Elizabeth Ann Hill

Cover illustration © Melvyn Warren-Smith by arrangement
with P.W.A. International Ltd.

The moral right of the author has been asserted

Published in Large Print 1998 by arrangement with Severn
House Publishers Ltd.

Magna Large Print is an imprint of
Library Magna Books Ltd.
Printed and bound in Great Britain by
T.J. International Ltd., Cornwall, PL28 8RW.

Author's Note

The book you are holding is one of two which were first published under the pen-name Anna Vivian, and I have been asked to tell you something of their history. As authors go, I was quite young when I wrote them and they bring back memories of what, for me, was a very exciting time. Also, like old diaries, they provide a glimpse of someone I used to be.

Last spring I read them again for the first time in many years and heard the 'voice' of a different person—a twenty-five year old, inexperienced but very eager to be that marvellous thing, an author. I had just won a short story competition in *Woman's Own* and had promptly decided this qualified me to move straight on and produce a book. Feeling that my own name didn't sound literary enough, I concocted a pseudonym, using my grandfather's middle name, Vivian.

The conventional wisdom is that you should write of what you know, but I paid no heed to that and plunged immediately into an historical novel. An odd choice indeed for someone who, in those days, read nothing but science fiction. However, beguiled by period costumes, I set to work. There were false starts, several of them; projects abandoned and later burned in sheer disgust. Nevertheless, I ploughed on, eventually finished *Remember Rachel* and sent it to a publisher. Lo and behold, it was accepted! Thrilled to bits, I then turned out *The Kendrick Girls* in what, for me, was record time. Both books have their faults, but I was learning my craft and delighted to see my apprentice efforts in print.

That was eighteen years ago. I'm now in the foothills of middle age and, inevitably, my work has evolved somewhat. When I am old (hopefully still *compos mentis* and still producing), my stories will no doubt be different again—which is as it should be. Unless they simply follow a formula, books tend to mirror their authors, so a writer who begins in youth and continues all through life is apt to leave, by way of her novels, a series of snapshots of herself.

The book in your hands is just such a snapshot. It was written with huge enthusiasm and a blithe self-confidence I've never since recaptured. I may have refined my style in later years, but I had enormous fun in writing these two novels. Those which followed were harder toil, so I do feel a certain nostalgia for those early days. I enjoyed the adventure of writing them, and I hope they will amuse and entertain you.

ONE

Barbara Kendrick rarely had dealings with failure. Her disappointments had always been small and infrequent. Perhaps that was why, when life delivered a double dose of defeat, she could not come to terms with it but responded instead with a reckless obsession that eventually cost three lives.

For as long as Abigail could remember, Barbara had been the great success, first in everything. Barbara was the pretty one. Barbara got top marks in school. She was invariably picked to present bouquets to visiting dignitaries, and naturally they heaped upon her such honours as the post of 'monitor' and later 'Head Girl'. Now and again she sang solos at parish concerts and the vicar once called her his favourite songbird. Barbara, in fact, had flourished from the very cradle on a diet of concentrated praise and admiration—and she reached adulthood armed with all the assurance that this can bring.

Between Barbara and her half-sister there existed an enmity that stretched back to their infancy. Barbara was two when Abigail was born, and all through the years of their growing up she had striven to keep her sister out of the limelight and out of daddy's affections. Her attempt to monopolize her father's love was hitherto Barbara's only real failure in life. Maybe that was why she loathed Abigail with such intensity.

Roland Kendrick was especially fond of his younger daughter, perhaps because she was so much like her mother, Sarah. If pressed, he would have to admit that he preferred his second wife for her kindness and her sense of fun—and Abigail had inherited both.

Barbara had resented his remarriage from

the time she was old enough to understand. Her own mother, a well-bred and fragile woman, had died when Barbara was eight months old. Within another six months Roland had married Sarah Spry, a common fisherman's daughter from 'down the hill' on the waterfront. Needless to say, Barbara hated her.

Small wonder therefore that the Kendrick sisters detested one another, although Abigail's feelings were less venomous and her sense of humour always served to dilute the animosity.

Barbara possessed that brand of sugar-coated nastiness that people are often apt to excuse in those who are physically decorative. Perhaps it was because the barbs were so ingenuously phrased and delicately delivered, because she smiled so often and so readily. Barbara was one of those who always appeared to observe convention and propriety—however improper her natural wants and instincts might be. And if she occasionally showed a little spite—well, people overlooked it because she was so attractive and such an asset at parties.

Of course, a thing of beauty is always displayed to best advantage against a plain background and that was why she chose Jessie as a best friend. Jessie Redmond was portly—a cherubic, sentimental little creature and guaranteed never to offer Barbara the slightest competition. She was a useful companion on shopping trips but apt to get in the way at parties.

On this Christmas Eve of nineteen hundred and five, Barbara was aged twenty-one and Abbie nineteen. Sarah had died a few years before, leaving Roland alone with his battling daughters. The old man, being a sociable soul, had arranged a dinner party for the girls and some of their friends, and he presided cheerfully over a table stacked with festive food.

Their guests included the plump Jessie, who wolfed her way with happy abandon through all eight courses and still had room for roasted chestnuts afterwards. Beside her sat a pale young man with thin, brown hair and a bit too much chin, who had come to gaze with love upon Barbara and absorb her every remark. He was one of her sadder victims and his name was Geoffrey. The lucky ones were those she demolished swiftly. Others, like Geoffrey, were allowed to linger on in hopeless devotion for months until she finally swatted them or simply forgot their existence.

The other guest that evening was everything Geoffrey envied and wished to be, the target of a dozen marriage-minded females. Every girl in the neighbourhood wanted him and, it was sourly agreed, Barbara Kendrick was odds-on favourite to get him. He was tall and strongly built, easy in his manner, with a kind of raffish humour which recommended him to Roland as a damn good sort for a son-in-law. He was blond and green-eyed and his name was Colin Wylie.

Barbara herself was confident that Wylie was hers for the taking. She thought it a law of nature that the most beautiful girl in town should capture the most popular man. It was only right and proper.

She had chosen this evening to offer him a little encouragement, certain that he would leap at the chance. The atmosphere seemed perfect for a swift, decisive conquest. Barbara had supervised the preparations in person and spent most of the day terrorizing the younger servants into an orgy of cleaning and polishing. It had certainly been worthwhile.

The lamps, fitted with pink glass shades, poured a rosy light over the room. In one corner a great fir tree stood, laden with baubles and tinsel. The table was spread with a white damask cloth, and for a centrepiece the maids had contrived a delicate wicker gondola, filled with damp mosses, ferns and Christmas roses. The silver, the Venetian glasses, the carafes of spring water and the dumpy, coloured candles set at intervals along the table provided a gorgeous setting for the meal.

Barbara had bedecked herself with equal care. She had chosen a dress of mauve silk, trimmed sparingly around the neckline with an embroidered leaf pattern in dark green. She was very much admired for her delicate features and finely textured skin—and yet she might have been improved, had some little irregularity lent character and warmth to her face. That evening she had piled her dark brown hair up into the latest style and completed the effect with a small silver comb. Everything was tasteful, everything matched.

Throughout the meal she smiled and chattered charmingly with Wylie across the table, carefully ignoring Abigail who sat on his left, excluding her from the conversation.

Abbie was short and undeniably tubby— no doubt because of her passion for peppermint creams and crystallized jelly fruits. With difficulty she had wrestled her hair into a quite fashionable style. It was light brown and stubbornly wiry. She thought it was insipid and it caused her almost as much grief as the scattering of freckles across her nose and checks. To atone for all this mediocrity, nature had given her startling blue eyes and a humorous disposition which Wylie happened to find very appealing.

Had Barbara known of this she would have been annoyed but not unduly worried. Men, she thought smugly, always married women for their looks, and it was unthinkable that she should have anything to fear from her sister in that respect. Abigail was merely a nuisance, never a threat.

'Well,' said Roland suddenly, glancing at his pocket watch, 'it's almost ten. I suggest we repair to the drawing room for an hour and then, when we've all quite recovered from Mrs Anstey's excellent dinner, we'll set out for St Andrew's. It's years since I've been to Midnight Mass. Think it's time I put in an appearance, don't you? What do you say? Shall we?'

They thought it a good idea. Barbara got up and Geoffrey leapt hopefully to his feet, only to be ignored. She turned to Colin, expecting his immediate attention, and was unpleasantly surprised to see that he was already leaving the room arm-in-arm with her sister. Barbara sniffed, assuming he was merely being civil, and grudgingly allowed the excited Geoffrey to escort her instead.

Jessie followed with Roland, her eyes gleaming at the thought of the row of chestnuts roasting by the fire in the drawing room. It was hardly surprising, therefore, that when they were preparing to leave for church, Jessie announced that she felt sick.

'Poor dear,' said Barbara sweetly, 'perhaps you should go upstairs and lie down.'

'If you'd rather, m'dear, you're welcome to stay the night,' added Roland. 'Spend the whole of Christmas with us if you like.'

Jessie groaned and gazed pitifully from one to the other. Her face had turned white and she perched uneasily on the edge of the sofa.

'If you don't mind I think I'd prefer to go home. My parents will be expecting me.'

'Naturally, yes. Quite right. Silly of me. Awfully sorry, m'dear. Hope it wasn't the pork that upset you.'

No, Daddy, just her disgusting appetite, thought Barbara, the smile never leaving her face.

Colin got to his feet. 'Come on, Jess, I'll take you home.'

'No!' said Barbara sharply. 'I mean ... Well, Geoffrey can do that.'

Geoffrey looked crestfallen.

'You don't mind, do you?' coaxed Barbara. 'And I believe that you and Jessie live quite near to each other. Isn't that right?'

'Yes, but I thought we were going to church,' he objected limply.

'Please. For me.'

Geoffrey weakened. 'If it's what you really want ...'

'There's a dear,' said Barbara briskly. 'I always know I can rely on you. Now come on. If we hang around much longer we'll miss the service.'

She allotted Geoffrey a brief kiss on the cheek and rang for the maid to fetch their coats.

'Poor devil,' murmured Abigail to Wylie. 'She treats him like an errand boy.'

'He shouldn't be such a fool,' replied Colin softly. 'I don't know why these gentle types always fall for a woman they can't handle. Any man who hopes to deal with Barbara will have to be a lot tougher than she is.'

'Is that so? And I suppose you think you could manage her?'

'I'm sure of it—but whether I would choose to do so is another matter.'

Abbie smiled faintly. She had heard that sort of talk before. Men who had set out to conquer Barbara generally ended up licking their wounds for months afterwards.

'Are you two ready?' urged Roland. 'Time we were off.'

Having got rid of Geoffrey's hovering presence, Barbara deftly manoeuvred herself between Colin and Abigail in church. She slid a glance at her sister's dress and smirked. It was apricot-coloured, much too bright—and it emphasized her plumpness.

Hardly suitable for church, Barbara thought, but then she's always had gaudy taste. Common, like her mother. That sort are all the same. She always laughs too loudly—and she tells jokes. Men don't like women who tell jokes. Of course, she's just trying to impress Colin.

During the service Barbara managed to misplace her hymnbook and found herself conveniently forced to share his—to remind him, as it were, of how nice it would be to share everything with her.

They left St Andrew's at a quarter past one and Wylie made his own way home.

He was twenty-eight, an architect who had just gone into practice on his own. He rented modest apartments on Colter Avenue. They suited him well enough but Barbara saw them as cramped and shabby. Needless to say, as soon as they were married she would expect him to move into Gypsy Hollow with her, for she had no intention of sharing a three-roomed flat.

With her usual self-confidence, Barbara was already laying plans for the rest of their lives; plans based on the mere assumption that she would acquire Colin as a matter of course. This had been the pattern of her life. To want something was to get it. She had no misgivings that this time was going to be any different—which was unfortunate because the coming spring held some serious disappointments for her.

The Kendrick family home was a three-storeyed house, built in a broad L-shape, with high ceilings, wide staircases and cumbersome oak furniture. The ground on which it stood was once common land, traversed by a public footpath. It was often used, not only by the people of Jennyport but also by bands of gypsies who favoured the area as a camping ground. When the land was fenced off in eighteen hundred and twelve, the house which was built there still retained the local placename of 'Gypsy Hollow'.

It boasted a spacious, south-facing study and library, plus an elegant dining room. Across the hallway was a vast lounge which was normally used for parties. The rusty-gold carpet could be taken up for dancing and there was comfortable seating for at least thirty people. Roland himself preferred the drawing room. It had an inglenook and he would retire to this glowing corner with a book each evening after dinner. The first floor offered five large bedrooms and the small apartments at the top of the house were occupied by the staff. Each room reflected subdued wealth and good taste, comfort and style without vulgarity.

The only sign of disorder at Gypsy Hollow was the garden. There were no neat flowerbeds, no carefully trimmed walks, no croquet lawn or sundial. Instead there was a profusion of unruly plant life. Matted and coiling, shrub and creeper interwoven, it grew to within six feet of the house on all sides. Amidst this free-for-all, the rhododendrons and azaleas had won most ground. They grew high and strong in the sunlight and blossomed brilliantly in spring. The grounds occupied the best part of six acres and were surrounded by a high stone wall, into which was set a pair of tall, wrought-iron gates.

Gypsy Hollow was not generally considered to be part of Jennyport. Half a mile of meandering country road lay between the house and the outskirts of that energetic little town. From the gates of the Kendrick residence the road wandered up a gentle slope, curved around a pair of ancient elms and began its descent to the sea.

The first houses, those at the top of the town, were solid, respectable, squarely middle-class. Here were the frilly curtains and the pot plants, the self-conscious, small success.

Further down were the shopping centre and places of entertainment. There were two theatres, a music hall, tennis courts, public gardens and, as a small, sad acknowledgement to Jennyport's past, a maritime museum.

Most of these houses and amenities had been built within the past thirty years, forming a bizarre expansion on the ancient fishing village—the original cluster of stone cottages still huddling defensively together around the quayside. These odd little dwellings with their boisterous inhabitants were Jennyport's own true self.

Dipping and weaving through alleyways and tiny courtyards, the streets of the old village were cobbled and crooked, in character with the jumbled, slanting little houses; some bravely colour-washed, others plain and sternly granite. No two were alike, yet most of them sported window-boxes or painted shutters. Many were over three hundred years old and all had a cheerfully unkempt appearance.

Thirty years had passed since the disappearance of the great shoals of pilchards that once provided Jennyport with her living. She was built to house the fishermen and had done so for generations. But now the fish were scarce, new people built fancy houses up on the hill and a sprinkling of city-dwellers arrived in summer—every year more of them. Jennyport had turned into a holiday town. Together with the borough of Wellanford, four miles distant, it had caught the attention of the touring public and would never be the same again.

Now only a few small mackerel boats still operated in the area. Twice a week they tied up at the quay to sell fish to the townspeople but the bulk of their catch would be sent to London for sale in the big markets. Most of the local men cast their lines purely for themselves and their families, bringing home just enough for a day or two.

Such a man was Sammy Spry. In fine weather he passed much of his time sitting out at the end of the quay, a bundle of withies at his side and his fingers busy with the making and mending of crab and lobster pots. At the age of sixty-five his hands still moved with the deft assurance that comes of a lifetime's practice. Abbie could remember sitting there beside her Uncle Sammy on summer evenings when she was quite small, watching him bend and twist those pliable lengths of willow in the same expert fashion.

Barbara had never understood her sister's wish to visit the old man, nor the pleasure she took in his company. Even now, as a grown woman, she paid him frequent calls, often taking a pie or a cake along with her.

When Colin and I are married, thought Barbara gleefully, and when Daddy dies, Abigail will find herself so unwelcome at Gypsy Hollow that she'll be glad to move in with old Spry for good. Anyway, it's where she belongs.

TWO

The tide was coming in fast. In half an hour the rock pools would be covered and small waves would be breaking over the shingle, bowling the pebbles up and down the slope as the water surged in and slithered back again, gaining a little ground with every new rush.

Abbie sat on a shelf of rock, her bare feet dangling in the water and the heavy skirt and petticoats pulled up around her knees as she watched a hermit crab swaying casually across the bottom of a pool.

This was her favourite cove. A mile and a half from town, enclosed by storm-beaten cliffs and with only a hazardous footpath leading down to it, this beach offered seclusion, a place to relax and to think. It was early March, a bright and chilly day, though Abbie was never one to feel the cold.

Her father had been seeming unwell lately. He was less jovial and increasingly tired. It was several weeks since he had taken one of his long walks—or even played a game of cards. If asked, he would say that he felt splendid, which was obviously untrue.

Abigail frowned as she wriggled her toes in the water. Why would he not be sensible and see a doctor? He had always distrusted the medical profession. It was just an eccentricity, of course, but one that a man of seventy could not afford.

'What are you scowling at?'

Abigail jumped. 'How did you know where to find me?'

'I ran into your Uncle Sammy,' said Colin, settling himself on the rock beside her. 'He says this is one of your haunts.'

'Hmm.' Abbie smiled. 'So it is. I discovered this place when I was about nine. The crowds never come here. Too far from town, no shops or pierrots to keep them entertained.'

'I caught you looking miserable just now. Had a fight with madam?'

'Barbara and I quarrel twice daily without fail. I don't let it upset me.'

'Then why the long face?'

'Haven't you noticed that Dad's not as perky as he used to be?'

Wylie shook his head.

'There's something wrong,' insisted Abigail. 'He gets out of breath so easily. I wish he'd see a doctor.'

'It's probably those damned cigars. He's never without one and—well, he is a bit ...'

'Fat,' finished Abbie. 'I know. Must be where I get it from.'

'I wouldn't call you fat exactly,' he mused, considering her figure. 'A bit generous, perhaps, but ...'

'How tactful.'

'... I'll find a way to work that off you once we're married.'

For a moment she didn't realize what he had said, then slowly she turned a startled face to him.

'What?'

'You're not going to make me say it again, are you?'

'You want to marry me? Whatever for?' Her voice rose in disbelief. 'I'm not good-looking like Barbara ...'

'True,' said Colin wickedly.

'Well, don't you prefer her? Don't you like her?'

'Barbara is variously admired, worshipped, coveted and so on by every male in town. I think you would be hard pressed to find one who actually likes her—although there are plenty who'd be foolish enough to marry the girl, if only for the kudos. Whoever she chooses in the end will probably be in for a very rough time.'

'I thought you said you could handle her.'

'Certainly, but what is the point in

signing on for a lifelong pitched battle? Barbara's no fun, Abbie. She takes herself too seriously. The lady believes she's the bee's knees and I find that rather tiresome.'

'You mean it, don't you?' breathed Abigail, a wide, happy grin lighting her face.

'Never been more serious. After all, we get on well together, don't we? You make me laugh—and anyway,' he screwed his face into a lecherous leer and slid an arm around her waist, 'I want somebody substantial to grab hold of in bed, m'dear.'

'When the corsets come off you might get more than you bargained for.'

'Oh, I've already made allowance for that.'

She punched him playfully. 'Beast.'

'How many children do you want?' he asked, getting up and offering a hand to help her down on to the shingle.

'Well, I've always wanted a big family—but I'll settle for six.'

'Good God, I'll have to work overtime.'

'I'd like four boys and two girls, I think.'

'I see I'm marrying a demanding woman, but you'll have to control yourself. Too much rough stuff and I'll be worn out before I'm thirty.'

'Not you,' scoffed Abbie. 'I've heard one or two things about you,' she added slyly.

'Rumours, lies and exaggerations.'

Colin had a reputation all right. One of those quiet, tantalizing reputations with a good deal of truth behind them. Perhaps it was because he had slept with some of the choicest women in town—many of them married—that he had learnt just how sadly their good looks compared with an amiable nature. Some of those doll-like, porcelain-perfect faces were accompanied by a similarly cold and brittle disposition.

They made their way back along the beach, following the tideline, along which was scattered the usual debris thrown up by a heavy sea. There were great heaps of the brown rubbery wrack that the local children called 'popper weed', plus cuttlebones, bits of frosty, half-crystallized quartz and the occasional mermaid's purse. Once, years before, Abbie had found a wedding ring in one of the rock pools. It was tarnished and scratched after years of tossing by the tide. Now, as she remembered that ring, it seemed almost prophetic.

'Shall we have a party to announce it?' she asked. 'A big party with everyone we know?'

'Of course.'

'Next Saturday?'

'Whenever you like, but nothing too formal or I'll have to hire a suit for the occasion.'

'True,' agreed Abigail, chuckling. 'I don't want them to think I'm marrying someone disreputable.'

'I promise to take a bath. I might even shave.'

For the moment Abbie forgot her sister and thought instead of the pleasure this news would bring to Roland.

'Dad will be thrilled when we tell him.'

'You think he approves of me?'

'I know he does and we must tell him straight away,' she said. 'Maybe it will buck him up a bit.'

The old man had never worried about Barbara's future, knowing that she was beset on all sides with offers of marriage. But Abbie, overshadowed and often neglected, caused him some concern and he was anxious to see her happily settled.

This problem occupied his thoughts more often than either of the girls ever guessed, and perhaps that was why he sought to ensure that Abbie would never find herself short of cash, should a husband fail to appear.

Roland Kendrick died that afternoon. He was alone in the library, leafing through a copy of 'Henry IV, part one' when the pain came, and suddenly he couldn't breathe. It took all of his strength to reach the bell cord and ring for the maid.

He was all but dead when she found him. While Abbie and Colin wandered contentedly across the beach, planning their lovely surprise for Dad, Gypsy Hollow was in uproar and the doctor was on his way.

It was four-thirty when they returned and found Dr Mackie's gig parked in the drive.

The door was opened by a very tearful housemaid and Mackie could be seen at the top of the stairs in quiet conversation with Barbara, who seemed uncommonly agitated.

Abbie called up to her. 'Barbara, what's happened? What's going on?'

Her sister turned away and disappeared across the landing, leaving the doctor to break the news. He came down the stairs and said quietly,

'I'm sorry, Miss Kendrick. Your father had a massive heart attack. He was dead before I arrived. Perhaps if he had consulted me some months ago it might have been prevented but you must understand that he'd been abusing his health for years. It may comfort you to know that the whole thing was over in less than five minutes.'

White and silent, Abbie stared at him.

'Just—like that?' She snapped her fingers.

The doctor nodded. 'Almost. And it's not such a bad way either. Far better than months of increasing disablement.'

'Of course,' she said faintly. 'Thank you.'

For the moment the loss of him seemed less important than the way in which he died. Her mother's last illness had been a lingering misery which made Roland's brief end easier to accept.

'Come in the drawing room and sit down,' Wylie said. Turning to the maid he added, 'Could you bring us some strong tea, Please? Oh, and what about Barbara—where is she?'

'In her room, sir. Says she doesn't want to see anybody yet. I think it frightened her—Mr Kendrick going suddenly like that, without any warning. I don't believe she realized just how bad his health was.'

'Too full of herself to notice,' muttered Abigail bitterly. 'And she wasn't so stricken when my mother died.'

'Come on, Abbie,' pressed Colin.

She followed him into the drawing room and sat down.

'Poor Dad. He enjoyed life so much—his food, his cigars, a good joke. And he always had an eye for the ladies. I think, when he was young, he must have been a bit like you. Funny thing, we had duck for dinner last night. It was his favourite and I thought, Well, what's life without a bit of pleasure? It's true he eats more than is good for him but he does so enjoy Mrs Anstey's roast duck. Somehow I suspect that, even if he'd known he was going to die, it wouldn't have spoilt his appetite.' She sighed. 'God, I wish we'd had time to tell him we're getting married. He would have been delighted.'

Wylie was thoughtful for a moment,

then he said, 'As things stand at the moment, Abbie, we'll have to postpone the announcement. Just for a few weeks. No one is going to feel like celebrating an engagement under the circumstances.'

'Yes, I suppose so, especially for Barbara's sake. She's had enough shocks for one day.'

As it happened, however, this family upset was soon to be compounded by a further surprise, one which would add another explosive factor to the Kendrick sisters' feud.

On a day soon after the funeral a small group of interested parties gathered in the drawing room at Gypsy Hollow for the reading of the will ...

'You robbed me!' Barbara's face was contorted with the kind of tearing rage that sometimes precedes murder. 'What did you say to him? What did you do to convince him ...? What lies did you tell him? Papa would never have done this to me unless you had a hand in it ...' Her voice rose to an ugly shriek.

Abbie took a few steps backwards. She had never before seen such a display of temper from her sister. It was as if every ounce of contempt, resentment and spite that Barbara had nurtured over the years had finally found release in this one appalling outburst.

'For God's sake, Barbara, I didn't know. I can't tell you why he did it. I'm more surprised than anyone.'

'Thief,' screamed Barbara, 'pilfering, underhanded little pirate!'

All of a sudden her voice cracked and she clutched at her throat.

Terrified, Abbie rang for the maid, convinced that her sister was about to follow Roland.

Heather came and took charge of the situation, seeming more annoyed than worried. She was a hefty, commanding woman of forty-one, supremely capable and toughened by the raising of thirteen brothers and sisters. Like another fractious infant, Barbara was firmly escorted upstairs to lie down.

'What's the matter with her?' asked Abbie, when the maid came back some twenty minutes later.

'Hysteria. She'll be all right. I gave her a drop of brandy and put her to bed. One of these days that temper will be the death of her, though I suppose it's not my place to say so. Don't you remember, Miss, when you and your sister were children and Mr Kendrick took you both to the fair? There was a costume doll on the hoop-la stall that Miss Barbara wanted—and you won it. Remember the tantrum? As I recall she finished up by fainting.'

Abbie could indeed recall something of the sort. 'Thank God it doesn't happen very often,' she muttered.

'Miss Barbara doesn't get thwarted very often,' pointed out Heather. 'Will that be all, Miss?'

'Um, yes,' said Abigail absently, 'and thank you for your help.'

'Pleasure, Miss. I'll make you some tea, shall I?'

'That would be lovely.'

Abbie sat down beside the hearth in the inglenook to ponder on what had happened. She was the main beneficiary in her father's will. There had been no equal split and no reason had been given for the terrific imbalance between the two bequests.

Clearly, Roland Kendrick was not guided by impartial fatherly love. His preference and concern for his youngest had crystallized as an eighty per cent share of his stocks, securities and other investments—although Gypsy Hollow itself now belonged jointly and equally to the two girls.

Barbara, mindful as always of her reputation, waited until the executor and other guests had left before cornering Abbie in the drawing room to express her feelings about the will.

Abbie put a hand to her forehead, as if to still the pulsing ache in her temples.

She understood that Roland's decision was a gesture of great affection—but she somehow wished he hadn't done it.

Gnawing at a deeper level was the knowledge that the quarrel was far from over, that it could only get worse. This blow had left Barbara reeling and Abbie feared that her forthcoming marriage to Colin would herald even greater hostilities. The announcement to which she had so looked forward now became a matter of dread.

In the end it was five weeks before she decided that her sister's feelings had been spared for long enough. It was presumptuous of Barbara to believe she had a claim to Wylie in the first place and so, one Tuesday morning, finding her sister alone in the lounge, Abbie took the opportunity of breaking the news. She had braced herself for a burst of hysterics but met instead with a tense and ominous calm that was even more alarming.

THREE

'We're going to announce it on Saturday. There'll be a party of course and,' Abbie struggled to conceal her anxiety, 'well, I do hope you'll come.'

She was standing with her back to the French windows and her sister sat stiffly on one of the plushy red settees beside the piano. Barbara's face was immobile, like something chipped from marble, and the grey-speckled eyes stared balefully into Abigail's.

'You're not—upset—are you?'

Barbara's mouth twitched into a tight smile. She looked strained and bloodless, grimly controlled.

'I'm very pleased for you,' she said evenly. 'Will it be a long engagement?'

'No. We thought perhaps September the

fifteenth for the wedding.'

'September. Yes. It's the month I would have chosen.'

Just perceptibly, Abbie gulped.

'I must think about a wedding present for you,' continued Barbara, still in the same flat tone. 'I'm afraid I can't afford anything too elaborate. You'll understand, of course.'

The pale eyes glittered and Abbie shrugged uncomfortably.

'You know I don't care about such things,' she said as lightly as she could.

'Quite. Well, what an eventful year we're having. Whatever next, I wonder?'

'I expect you'll be married, too, before long. After all, you've got the whole town to choose from.'

'So I have. I can take my pick from what's left.'

Abigail felt a stab of annoyance at that. Her sister spoke of those unfortunate men as if they were seconds at a spring sale—substandard.

'Chris Gilley, for instance. He's good-looking and fairly well off,' blundered Abbie.

'Are you going to be charitable, dear, and arrange a compensation prize for your spinster sister? Will there be dinner parties with a selection of suitable candidates? Would you like to get me married off and out of the house?' The acid began to seep into Barbara's voice and the loathing on her face was now unmistakable.

'Look,' said Abbie hotly, 'I was only trying to help.'

'Don't patronize me. You don't really think you've scored over me, do you? You cannot honestly believe that Colin has chosen you for your own sweet self?'

'I know he has.'

'Oh, grow up,' snapped Barbara. 'He's after your money. You inherit the major portion of Daddy's stocks and securities— and suddenly Colin wants to marry you. Believe me, if the estate had been split evenly—fairly—he'd never have chosen you.'

Nothing, it seemed, could puncture Barbara's vanity. She could certainly see no fault in herself. If Roland had altered his will, it must have been because Abbie tricked him into it, and if Colin wanted to marry her then the reason could be expressed in pounds, shillings and pence. Naturally he would have preferred her elegant sister and no doubt he was chafing at the prospect of life with a plain and stupid wife.

'Don't be insulting.' Abigail's temper started to rise. 'You've no right to suggest he's mercenary.'

'Naturally you won't want to face facts,' said Barbara sweetly, 'when they're so unflattering.'

'You can tell yourself whatever you please if it's balm to your vanity, but let me make it clear that Colin proposed to me weeks ago—on the day that Dad died—and long before the will was read. He couldn't possibly have known what I would get. I didn't know it myself.'

Barbara's gaze wavered for an instant. There was the merest flicker of uncertainty that creased her brow and was swiftly gone.

'Liar.'

Abbie shook her head slowly and intently, her eyes fixed on those of the other girl.

Barbara smiled, composed once more, rescued by the old conceit. 'I don't believe you.'

Abigail sniffed. 'It hardly matters what you believe, but if we are all to live together in this house there will have to be some kind of truce.'

'I have no intention of moving out if that's what you're hoping for.'

'I hadn't even considered it,' snapped back Abigail. 'I'm simply saying that we'll have to come to terms with each other if we're not to turn Gypsy Hollow into a battleground.'

The other raised an eyebrow and said nothing.

'Are we agreed? No trouble, no more arguments? I'm not the angry one, Barbara. It's you who are causing all the tension.'

'That is because I am the one who has suffered the grievances.'

'I don't expect you to like the situation, but let's not turn it into a feud or make life hell for Colin. He doesn't deserve that.'

'You needn't worry, little sister,' said Barbara, getting to her feet. 'I won't upset your marriage. As you so rightly say, I have the whole town to choose from and at least I shall never have to worry that some man is marrying me for my fortune—because I no longer have one, do I?'

Wearily, Abbie watched the door close behind her. The sooner Barbara found a man—preferably a rich one—to soothe her pride, the happier life would be for everyone.

Sammy Spry's cottage was one of those set solidly on the quayside, facing straight out to sea. Only a strip of cobbled walkway separated the houses from the harbour wall. When the tide was low and the wind onshore, a light powdering of fine, white sand would find its way indoors so that the women were forever sweeping it out again.

The upstairs windows looked out upon a broad expanse of bay, bordered on the east side by a jagged headland and on the other by a sprawling arm of green land which tapered with deceptive gentleness down to the sea. This was Pelaze point. Abbie had twice seen a ship go down out there—and in time she would see a third.

Today, however, she was absorbed with the happier business of her wedding. It had been a short engagement and the preparations were so many that she had almost forgotten the need for someone to give her away. Sammy had been delighted at the news and she knew he could be persuaded to do the honours—besides which, she needed his advice concerning a certain disreputable aunt.

'Well, now, I've never had to do anything like that before, not having any daughters of my own.' Sammy looked dubious. 'What do I have to say?'

'Hardly anything. Just walk me down the aisle and say that you're giving me to be married.'

'That's all?'

Abbie nodded. 'Please, Sammy.'

'Oh, of course, of course. It's just that I might look a bit awkward tussed up in a Sunday suit among all those fine people.'

'I can't remember any time or any situation when you've looked out of place. Anyway, it's been my experience that some of those fine people aren't worth much. It won't be a big wedding, you know. About thirty or forty guests.'

'When's it to be, then?'

'Three weeks on Saturday.'

'And what time must I be there?'

'Say, ten-thirty at Gypsy Hollow.'

Sammy nodded. 'Right you are.' His

brown, crinkled face suddenly creased into a broad smile. 'Sarah's girl getting married,' he murmured, mostly to himself. 'How the years slip out from under us! I'd never stopped to think that you were a grown woman, Abbie. I suppose we don't notice till such times as this. Makes me feel old—almost.'

'You don't seem old to me. I've seen men of thirty less fit than you.'

'That's true. Yes, it's true. I still do a full day's work and put food on the table.' He gestured round the kitchen-cum-sitting room that formed the ground floor of his cottage. 'Can't say I keep things too tidy, though.'

Sammy's house was always littered with the gear and trappings of a man who spent his life around boats—ropes, tarpaulins, odd spars of timber. Along one wall was stretched an old seine net, long disused but kept as a reminder of times past. There were oilskins tossed carelessly across chairs and in one corner a pair of leather sea boots. On the table before him lay part of an old oar handle, surrounded by a pile of shavings. It amused him to carve toy boats and wooden dolls for the neighbours' children.

He was tough and he was generous and Abbie had always brought her worries to him. Not even Roland had possessed the same comfortable grip on life. Sammy was content and at peace within his own mind—with an odd capacity for spotting the unrest in other people's.

He picked up his knife and began whittling away at the oar, his cap tipped slightly to one side and the springy white hair straying out around it.

'What about your Aunt Ivy?' he said, not looking up. 'Will you be asking her to the wedding?'

Abbie bit her lip and looked sheepish.

'Do you think I should?'

'Oh, it's not for me to say. She's my sister, of course. Your mother's sister and your own blood kin. But she'll spoil your wedding, my love. You know that, don't you?'

The girl sighed. 'Yes. I was going to ask you what I should do.'

'I know but you must decide for yourself. I'll say this, though—whatever choice you make, I won't call it the wrong one.'

He winked at her and Abigail grinned. Left to her own devices she would conveniently forget Aunt Ivy. Sammy, knowing his sister, was not about to condemn Abigail for leaving her off the guest list.

She leaned across and kissed the old man's cheek.

'I'd better go now. I've got to pick up some shoes for the bridesmaids.'

She was greatly relieved that Sammy understood her feelings about Aunt Ivy. Abigail was no snob—but Ivy Whickle was undeniably an embarrassment. A widow, she lived alone in an ill-kept cottage in the village of Hallenhawke, six miles inland.

Jealous and quarrelsome, Ivy had little in

common with her good-humoured relatives in Jennyport. She gobbled her food and was wont to belch thunderously after a good meal. Loud-mouthed at the best of times, she became disgusting when drunk and would make vulgar suggestions to any man within earshot.

It was fortunate for Abigail that her aunt didn't figure too largely in her life. Ivy preferred her home ground, much to everyone's relief, and very little was heard from her.

However, her appetite was matched by a rapacious love for money. Barbara bore this in mind when seeking out ways to make mischief, and decided it might be a good idea to inform the grubby old woman of her niece's inheritance.

FOUR

Barbara detested Hallenhawke. Tired and sullen, cocooned in its age and its silence, the village seemed always wrapped in a kind of heavy stillness. The place was ancient and backward beyond redemption, with nothing to offer but its torpid calm.

The corn mill had closed in eighteen ninety-eight. Soon afterwards the foundry, too, had ceased its work of making turfing irons and farm implements. No industry had ever flourished in Hallenhawke.

She stopped outside the church, hesitated, then went inside for a few minutes. Some elusive instinct questioned the wisdom of what she was doing and she needed time to collect her thoughts before confronting Ivy Whickle.

The door banged shut behind her and

the heels of her fashionable boots clicked sharply on the flagstones as she walked down the central aisle. The place was deserted and there was a damp, powdery smell, like a curious cross between mildew and dry rot.

She sat down on a front pew and picked up a hymnbook. The leather cover was limp and cracked, the pages grubby. She flipped them idly through her fingers, her mind on other things.

Churches, weddings. Her gaze fell on the altar and a hard coil of bitterness began to twist inside her. There would be flowers at St Andrew's. Great baskets and sprays of flowers, a choir, an admiring congregation with all eyes on the central figure—Abigail. What a waste!

Barbara shook herself and glanced around her, unable to imagine a similar scene in this setting. This was a church for grim spiritual business where the vicar hurled weekly doses of guilt and humility at his flock. Barbara sniffed. She had never,

57

thank God, been much afflicted with either of those. Then she remembered the matter in hand and took comfort in the hope that Ivy's presence at the wedding might prove something of a blot on Abigail's great day.

Barbara got up and left the church, making her way briskly down the deserted road, past the row of cottages that stood beside the stream. The last but one belonged to Ivy Whickle. Barbara knocked twice and, getting no answer, lifted the latch and stepped inside.

Sombre would best describe the room in which she stood. The floor was uneven and sloped a little, several degrees off the level. There was a wooden table, a bulky Welsh dresser displaying the old woman's crockery, two hard chairs and a glass-fronted cupboard containing bags of flour, bunches of dried herbs, some tea canisters and other basic supplies.

A real witch's kitchen, she thought with distaste, noting the high-backed wooden bench seat by the hearth and the kettle boiling on its tripod over the fire.

Outside she heard the clank of a pail, set down heavily on the back doorstep. Ivy had spent the past half-hour swopping venom with the peat-cutter's wife down at the pump.

The door opened and a small, wiry woman with matted hair and a narrow, down-curving mouth stepped inside. She had a sinewy, aggressive look, like a rather peevish stoat.

'What do you think you're doing here? Just walked in, did you?'

The voice was scratchy and well befitted its owner.

'I tried knocking. I thought I would come in and wait, seeing there was no answer.'

'Hmmph.'

'Do you know who I am?'

'Oh,' Ivy grunted. 'Yes. The sister. Belinda, is it?'

'Barbara.'

Ivy looked her up and down, a resentful flicker of the eyes, taking in the details of Barbara's suit. It was a subtle, rusty-brick colour, set off by a cream blouse and gloves, plus a perched hat. The old woman didn't attempt to hide her envy.

'So what may a fine person like you want with me?'

'I was just passing and I wondered if ... Well, may I sit down for a while?'

Ivy shrugged and Barbara selected the more sturdy of the two chairs.

'Comfortable? I suppose now you'd like some tea?'

Barbara eyed the grubby crockery and declined.

'You are aware, no doubt, that my father passed away some months ago?'

'I heard.'

'But you may not know of the eccentric way in which he divided his property.'

Mrs Whickle heaped a couple of spoonfuls of tea into the pot and poured on some hot water.

'Why should I? He was nothing to me. You're not going to tell me that I've been left a fortune?'

Barbara smirked. 'No. But your niece has.'

'Eh?'

'Daddy was somewhat over-generous toward Abigail in his will. I assume your brother Samuel has benefited to some extent. I wondered if you, too, had been informed.'

Ivy listened, riveted. Behind the darting eyes an equally busy brain was computing all the implications of Barbara's news.

'How much has she got?'

'A very great deal—even by my standards.'

Ivy exhaled slowly and sat down to pour some of the brew into a chipped old cup with no handle.

'Nobody told me.' She sounded very piqued indeed.

'How strange! How unfair!'

Mrs Whickle sucked noisily at her tea,

regarding the young woman over the rim of her cup.

'I believe everyone else was informed of the situation immediately. Perhaps they simply forgot you.'

Ivy set her cup down with a bang and the pallid liquid spattered across the table top.

'They're cheating me, cutting me out—as usual.'

'Maybe they were simply too concerned with the wedding ...'

'What wedding?' snapped Mrs Whickle.

'Good Lord! Didn't they tell you that either? Abigail is to be married in two weeks' time. St Andrew's, eleven forty-five on Saturday the fifteenth of September.'

'Who's she marrying? I thought it would take her years to land a husband, being so plain as she is.' With her instinct to hurt, the old woman paused for a sly dig at Barbara. 'But she certainly beat you to it. Why's that, I wonder?'

'Money is a fair substitute for beauty.'

Ivy could see the logic in that.

'Who is he?'

'A Mr Wylie. Colin Wylie.'

'Colin, is it? There's a pretty and delicate name for a man. What does he do?'

'He's an architect.'

'I see. Sounds like an impressive creature.'

'Anyway,' went on Barbara, 'as you've obviously not received an invitation, would you like me to mention the matter to Abigail? Remind her, so to speak?'

The old woman snorted. 'Don't trouble yourself. I don't need any invitation. Couldn't read it anyway,' she added. 'Never went to school.'

'Oh dear! Such a handicap.'

'Doesn't mean I'm stupid though.'

'Good heavens, no!'

'For instance,' said Ivy evilly, ' 'tis plain to me that you didn't come here with my welfare in mind. 'Tis more likely you hope to make trouble for your sister.'

'I merely thought you should know

what's happening.'

'Hah! If Abbie did specially well out of the old man's will, then it follows that you did badly. It's spite that's brought you here.' She was grinning broadly, crouched and leaning aggressively across the table. Her teeth were like her crockery: chipped and stained. 'If you're so keen to have me there, perhaps I should charge you for my trouble.'

'I'm sure you will wish to attend, with or without a—gift—from me.'

'Well I don't know about that. Not having any fine dresses to wear ...'

'I don't suppose Abigail would mind.'

'... and then there's the matter of travelling six miles either way, and a present for the couple. I'm a poor woman, remember?'

After a brief hesitation, Barbara opened her purse, took out the sum of ten guineas and handed it to Mrs Whickle.

'For your expenses. And no doubt the generous spread of food and drink at the reception will more than justify the trip.'

The cool eyes surveyed Ivy with quiet scorn as she counted the money and thrust it into a greasy apron pocket.

'Naturally you won't mention the fact that I invited you. Abbie might think it presumptuous of me, but I couldn't stand by and see you slighted. Are we agreed?'

'Aye, that's fair enough since you've done me a favour in coming here. If Abigail's a rich woman then I'll not let her forget her old auntie.'

'Quite,' beamed Barbara, satisfied.

Had she known Ivy better, she would have realized that promises made when sober could be wiped from the old woman's memory by a single glass of wine.

'Eleven forty-five, you said? On the fifteenth?'

'Yes. You won't be late, I trust?'

'I wouldn't miss a minute of it.'

'Good.' Barbara got up and the old woman followed her to the door. 'The more the merrier, don't you think?'

Ivy sneered as she watched the girl disappearing up the path. Sly little cat with her fine manners.

In good spirits, Barbara walked on up to the bend in the road where the driver was waiting for her, quietly cursing on the woman who had kept him hanging around for nearly an hour. He helped her up and the trap pulled away on its rattling journey back to town.

Even in summer there was something oppressive about this stretch of countryside. Here and there were great raw patches in the ground, caused by the cutting of peat. Elsewhere the land was scarred by swaling, burnt black and dotted with the charred stumps of gorse bushes. To see it smoking when the fire had passed, it was hard to believe that new growth would follow, fresher and stronger than before.

On all sides of Hallenhawke the ground sloped gently upwards to a series of hilltops. The most prominent of these was Maelan Carn. This gaunt outcrop of rock, riven and worn by driving rain and winter frost, always seemed closer than it really was. At the summit the stones reared up in stark outline against the sky—the bare bones of the landscape rising above the heather and bracken which grew farther down. It was a melancholy place at the best of times and the feeling grew stronger when the mist came down, ringing the hilltops and creeping in the valleys, the little grey droplets settling and soaking into the ground, dampening both the land and the mood of the people who lived there.

Only twice before had Barbara found cause to travel this road. Perhaps that was why she had never noticed the solitary house and garden half a mile south of Maelan Carn. And perhaps too, had her devious errand not taken her to Hallenhawke that day, she might never have met Ralph Allington.

Beside the road, some ten yards from the garden gate, was propped a roughly painted sign: *'Fresh brown 4½ d a dozen.'*

'Would you stop, please.'

The driver pulled up and helped her out of the trap.

'I won't be long.'

She walked up to the house and knocked.

A thin, dark woman answered the door. She was little more than five feet tall. Her hair was black, waist-length and poker straight, roughly fastened at the back with a tortoiseshell comb.

'Yes?'

'I'd like some of your eggs.'

'Oh. Right. Come in.'

Barbara followed her inside and waited in the sitting room while the woman went out to the hen coop.

'A dozen?' she called over her shoulder.

'Two dozen, I think. I'm very fond of brown eggs.'

'Right you are.'

The room was shaded and old-fashioned but unquestionably neat. A bracket clock occupied the mantelpiece. It looked expensive, as did the carpet, and yet the cushions and curtains appeared to be home-made. Nothing matched and there was a curious blending of quality and rubbish. Stranger still was the assortment of mechanical toys—automatons as they were called—crowded together on the sideboard.

Barbara frowned and glanced towards the back door. There was no sign of the woman. She sidled across the room for a closer look.

There were twirling ballerinas and juggling clowns, a squat and quite ridiculous-looking penguin in a bowler hat, soldiers presenting arms, a goblin playing a fiddle, and many others. Some of them were probably valuable. She picked up the penguin and turned it over in search of the key.

'They're my husband's.'

Barbara jumped and flushed with guilt.

'He collects them,' said the woman,

handing her the eggboxes. 'Daft, isn't it?'

'I suppose it's just another hobby.' Barbara smiled awkwardly. 'Men are natural collectors, aren't they?'

'Hmm. Mine is. He collects everything within reach.'

'I, uh, didn't know there was a farm here.'

'It isn't a farm. I just keep chickens. That'll be ninepence, by the way.'

Barbara handed her the money.

'They're fine thank you, Mrs ...'

'Allington.'

'Have you been here long? I don't often come this way, but ...'

'Nearly three years,' interrupted the woman brusquely. 'My husband is a Londoner but I prefer the country.'

Her manner, energetic and slightly impatient, went well with the pointed features and sharp, dark eyes. There was something perceptive and, yes, tough, about Mrs Allington. Barbara decided she didn't like her.

'Of course. Well, thank you again.'

The front door slammed and Mrs Allington raised an eyebrow.

'There he is. Late as usual.'

Barbara encountered the spouse in the hall and thought him unremarkable. She would have placed his age at somewhere around thirty. He was one of those infernally average people composed of medium height, medium brown hair, ordinary voice and round, unmemorable face, except—ah yes, there is always a magic, saving factor—he had a lovely, almost ecstatic smile. And there was confidence, too. His clothes, of good quality and carefully matched, bespoke a degree of self-love that appeared to be absent in his wife.

Barbara bid him a civil 'Good day' on her way out. She was not sufficiently interested to stop and exchange pleasantries and so failed to notice the intensity of his stare. Nor did she realize that he watched her all the way down the path and that his eyes followed the trap until it was out of sight.

His wife regarded him cynically for a moment or so, then, 'Ralph!'

He gave a start. 'All right, all right.'

'Get a move on with those groceries if you want to be fed on time.'

The man ambled into the kitchen and dumped the shopping bags on the table.

'Is it paid for?'

He looked wounded. 'Yes, of course.'

'All of it?'

'For God's sake, Primrose. You know I don't do—that sort of thing—any more.'

'Hmmph,' responded Mrs Allington. 'Only for lack of opportunity. And get those stupid toys off the sideboard. That woman noticed them. Put them up in the attic with your other junk—if you can find room.'

'Who was she?'

'Oh, just somebody wanting eggs. I didn't ask her name.'

FIVE

Colin and Abigail were married on a cool, cloudy morning in September and returned to Gypsy Hollow for the reception amidst flurries of rice and fussing relatives.

Eclipsed and forgotten, Barbara sought out her best friend, for Jessica was neither observant nor bitchy and would never notice her turmoil. Sad to say, Jessie didn't realize the need for tact, either.

'It was a lovely service! I adore weddings.'

'Mmph.'

'Abbie looks quite beautiful. Oh, isn't she lucky?'

'Luck,' said Barbara sourly, 'has nothing to do with it.'

'I never dreamed that she and Colin ... Well, just fancy! You never can tell, can you?'

Barbara glared at her friend. 'Isn't it time for another assault on the buffet table? Wouldn't you like a trifle or a leg of pork?'

'Oh, it's all right. I've got something.' Jessie flourished a vol-au-vent and a glass of champagne. 'You don't look too bright, you know. Eaten too much?'

Barbara gasped and rounded on her savagely. 'You're not only stupid, but cheeky, too.' She flounced off and Jessica shrugged. Barbara had always been unpredictable.

The reasons for her ill-temper were twofold: firstly the occasion itself and secondly her failure to spoil it, for there was no sign of Ivy Whickle.

All through the service Barbara had waited hopefully for the appearance of that disreputable figure. No Ivy. The old harridan had not only let her down but cheated her of ten guineas into the bargain. Now the reception was well under way and it seemed unlikely that Mrs Whickle would turn up at this late stage.

In the lounge the French windows were open to let in the air. Maids scurried to and fro with trays of snacks and dainties. One of the guests was trying out some popular tunes on the piano, and above the conversation and laughter Barbara didn't hear the insistent rapping of the front door knocker. Nor did she spot the spindly figure and surly face of Abigail's aunt when she pushed her way past the maid and sidled into the lounge.

Sammy was the first to see her as she elbowed her way through the crowd in search of her niece. A bolt of anger and dismay tore through him. Everything had gone so well for Abbie and now, like a wicked fairy, Ivy had come to upset her. But maybe, after all, something could be done. Quickly he put down his glass of ale and went after her.

Ivy, peering irritably about the room, turned round in answer to a tug at her sleeve and glared at Sammy Spry.

'Where's Abbie? I want to see her.'

He took his sister by the arm and pulled her towards the door. 'This way, Ivy.' As he dragged her out she managed to seize a handful of sandwiches and a bottle of sherry off the sideboard.

'What are you doing? Where are we going?' she squawked as he bundled her up the stairs.

'You want to see Abbie, don't you?'

'Yes, but ...'

'Well come on then.'

'Let me go. You'll tear me dress. It's new. I bought it special.'

Sammy glanced with distaste at her outfit. It was a glaring shade of purple and a good deal too big for her.

He hurried her along the landing, found a bedroom door with a key in it, thrust her inside and swiftly locked it.

There was a moment's puzzled silence within, followed by a torrent of thumping and swearing. Sammy heard a step and turned to find Heather standing beside him.

'It's Abigail's aunt,' he panted.

'Oh, yes, I know who she is. I'm surprised they invited her.'

'They didn't. I don't know what she's doing here but I'm not going to let her embarrass Abbie and spoil her party.' He handed the key to Heather. 'Think you can keep her in there for an hour or two?'

'As long as they don't hear her downstairs. She's kicking up a fair old row.'

'They're making plenty of noise themselves. Anyway, she's got a bottle of something or other. If we're lucky she'll drink the lot and pass out.'

Heather chuckled. 'Don't you worry now. I've dealt with worse than her.'

Sammy didn't doubt that for one moment and he returned to the lounge much relieved.

The hammering and cursing grew fainter. Heather waited a while longer until finally there was silence. It was, she thought, perhaps unfortunate that the bedroom

Sammy had chosen belonged to Miss Barbara.

And a very fine bedroom it was, decorated in shades of blue. Ivy sat down heavily on the bed and opened the bottle. She took a swallow and made a face. Dry sherry. Not exactly her favourite but apparently all she was going to get.

Curiously she eyed the brocade curtains and ran a hand over the quilt. It felt like satin. The carpet looked expensive and the furniture was all part of a matching set. Not an odd piece anywhere.

Ivy sneered. Everything so rich, so soft—and so fancy. A glint of crystal caught her eye, the perfume bottles on Barbara's dressing table. She got up and scuttled across for a closer look. There was a brush and comb set with silver backing and a number of tiny porcelain pots containing powder, hair pins and so on. Very dainty.

Her attention turned to the cupboards and drawers. Silk stockings, corsets and combinations flew into the air as Ivy busily turned out Barbara's belongings. She examined these lacy contrivances one by one, snorted, and tossed them away.

The wardrobe was a source of great interest. Mrs Whickle peered inside, rummaging through the dresses on the rail, finding colourful silks, quality skirts in broadcloth and mohair, a tweed top coat and numerous delicate fabrics for evening wear. There were carven hair-combs and velvet bows, a dark green evening cape trimmed with feathers, plus a pair of embroidered satin shoes. There seemed no end to the finery and Ivy was suddenly taken with a desire to try it on.

She gobbled the sandwiches, barely tasting them, and reduced the sherry to the halfway mark before setting to work.

Off came the purple dress and the ancient flannel drawers beneath, followed by a grimy cotton vest. She scooped up a pair of combinations from the floor and struggled into them. A brief experiment with a corset proved disappointing, for she couldn't manage the laces, and so she progressed to the more interesting business of choosing a dress. After much dithering she whipped a yellow satin concoction off its hanger and pulled it awkwardly over her head. A few contortions, with much panting, and she managed to fasten some of the buttons.

Ivy stood before the mirror to consider the effect. It needed something. She seized a straggling tuft of hair and pinned it up with a pink velvet bow. With the green feathered cape thrown across her shoulders for the final touch, Ivy was satisfied. She pranced and she twirled, curtseyed and simpered, then flung off the cloak and ripped at the dress buttons as she searched through the wardrobe for another.

By the time she had emptied the sherry bottle, all but one of Barbara's outfits lay strewn across the room.

Ivy reached for the last dress. It was satin, lavishly embroidered, of palest, peachy pink. It was, moreover, Barbara's favourite. Mrs Whickle pulled it on, tugged it down over her scrawny body and thought it very fetching.

Squatting before the dressing table, she found a hairpiece and pinned it atop her own grizzled locks, adding a spray of red feathers at either temple. Clouds of powder settled on the carpet and furniture as she patted the puff extravagantly over her face. The picture was completed by two livid dollops of rouge and all the jewellery she could find. There, finished. Perfect.

Such a shame that no one would see it, thought Ivy, swaying before the mirror. If only she could get out.

Heather had returned to the kitchen as soon as Ivy went quiet. Nearly an hour passed before she remembered the captive upstairs and thought it might be wise to look in on her.

Sprawled sullenly upon the quilt, Mrs Whickle was instantly alert at the sound of the key being fitted into the lock. She hopped off the bed and skittered across to hide behind the door.

Heather peeped into the room and, seeing no Ivy, ventured a few steps inside. Shoved squarely from behind, she tumbled forward and landed painfully on the carpet, while the old woman bolted across the landing and down the stairs, heading for the music, the food and the champagne.

'Dear God, who's that?' somebody whispered, and several pairs of eyes turned curiously upon the apparition in the doorway. A hush spread swiftly over the lounge and Ivy preened herself at what she took for admiration.

Abbie clapped a hand to her mouth and Colin looked at her enquiringly. 'Do you know ...?'

'Oh, my God,' breathed the bride, and Sammy despairingly closed his eyes.

'Where's my friend Belinda?' Ivy's voice lashed across the room.

Nobody budged. Nobody spoke. Behind a group of gentlemen guests, Barbara began edging towards the French windows. Ivy tottered up to the buffet table and seized a glass of champagne. Then her gaze fell on Colin.

'Oh my, ain't he handsome?' She curtseyed and leered at him. 'You're what I call a fine bit of goods. Lovely all over, dear. Everything a girl needs.'

A gust of laughter shook through him and he raised his glass to her. 'How very kind,' he said amiably.

'I've always liked big men. Too many midgets around these days—little short-arsed weeds with no stamina.'

Abigail stood rigidly beside her husband. She felt cold and faintly dizzy. This was just too awful.

Mrs Whickle winked at her. 'Don't you waste him, now. Plenty of bed and bouncy-cuddle keeps 'em happy. I should know. My old man was ecstatic all his life—till he got pneumonia and died.'

There was muffled disapproval from the ladies but Colin's grin broadened.

'Fancy letting him get cold enough to catch pneumonia.'

Ivy screamed with mirth. 'Oh, he's nice, he is. I like him.'

Abbie was on the verge of tears when her aunt suddenly caught sight of Barbara sliding quietly through the French windows.

'There she is!'

Barbara stiffened and the people drew back to allow Ivy past.

'This is my friend, who pays me social calls at home. Isn't that right, dear?'

Everyone stared.

'She's good to me,' confided Ivy loudly. 'Just two weeks ago she gave me ten guineas. Ten guineas, if you please! And she lets me wear her clothes. I call that generous, don't you?'

They still stared.

'Don't you?' repeated Ivy stridently, clamping an arm round the shrinking Barbara's waist.

A few people nodded obediently.

'Leave me alone,' hissed the girl, flinging her off. 'Go and talk to Abigail,' she whispered angrily. 'That's what you're here for.'

'Oh, high and mighty! Oh dearie me, it's all snot and dignity now, is it? Makes a difference when there's company, I suppose.'

She minced up and down in a bizarre imitation of Barbara's own gliding walk, feathers waving, bracelets clinking. She tossed her head haughtily and the hairpiece slipped down over one ear.

'Or are you just tetchy because I'm late? It's not my fault the horse threw a shoe ...'

'Will someone please remove this drunken person?' Barbara's voice trembled.

'I'll go when I'm ready,' announced Mrs Whickle. 'You're a cruel woman to bring me all this way and then chuck me out. I shall never invite you to tea again.'

At that moment she saw Heather bearing down on her and tried to escape through the crowd, but was caught and propelled from the room with much wriggling and cursing.

There was a ripple of comment. One or two women looked at Barbara and sniggered. From one corner came a burst of honest mirth—it was Wylie—and the amusement spread throughout the assembly until all were laughing, except one.

Barbara at last managed to slip away and fled to the privacy of her bedroom, there to find the ruin of her precious wardrobe.

'Who was that old girl?' Colin asked his wife.

'My aunt,' whispered Abbie, shame-faced.

'Your aunt?'

'My sister,' nodded Sammy. 'I'm sorry, I suppose we should have warned you about her.'

'Why? I think she's a character. We should have her round more often.'

'Lord forbid,' muttered Abigail. 'You

86

don't think she's upset anyone?'

'Upset them? Best bit of entertainment they've had in ages, and believe me, the joke is firmly on your sister.'

He was right, of course. The guests left some time later, thanking the Wylies for a highly enjoyable party, and no one really seemed aware of who Ivy Whickle was.

For Barbara, this was the latest in a chain of defeats and humiliations—but it did have a cautionary effect. It would never do to let people see how bitterly she felt about the marriage. There were many who would revel in her embarrassment and Barbara was not about to give them any further cause for talk.

And yet the trouble was only just beginning. She had done herself a greater disservice than she knew in seeking out Ivy Whickle. The old woman was one of those baneful acquaintances who, once encountered, have a way of returning to touch one's life with misfortune every so often.

SIX

Barbara knew from the start that living in the same house with the Wylies was going to be difficult. It proved, in fact, to be a nightmare of chafing envy. And yet to all appearances she was having a glorious time. Her social life, always busy, became positively hectic. With Colin married, her men friends thought their chances greatly improved. They called frequently, persistently. There were always bunches of roses and even the occasional home-grown poem. She thanked them sweetly and despised their offerings, for the notion still remained that Colin Wylie was rightfully hers and that sooner or later she would get him back.

It is probably one of the oldest truths that people always want what they can't have and, as the weeks wore on, Barbara's resentment hardened into something painful and tormenting that sapped the enjoyment from life and kept her awake at night.

She had heard tales of Colin's earthy talents between the sheets and always assumed that she would get the full benefit of them. The idea of sleeping with him had always fascinated her. She wanted to know what he was like—but that privilege had fallen to her sister.

Sometimes, in the small hours, she heard giggles and thumping noises from their room and she would lie with gritted teeth, her fingers clenching and clawing at the coverlet, her mind focused with malign intensity upon her sister, as if by force of will she could strike her dead. But of course these measures served only to give Barbara a headache. The hatred festered in her like a witch's brew, for what began as wounded vanity had become an obsession.

This boxed-in fury was all the more

exhausting because she seldom gave any outward sign of it. Pride forbade her to show the rage and demanded instead a bland indifference which cost her unending tension. There was the odd moment of release, of course—a bolt of sarcasm, public disclosures of Abbie's little failings, but always with a smile, always indirect.

For Abigail these were the brightest days of her life, times of laughter and long, cosy nights with her husband. In years gone by she had spent too many evenings alone, reading or sewing, while her sister was whirled from theatre to restaurant to music hall by an endless procession of besotted men. Abbie's life had long been a social void and, as if he recognized this deprivation, Colin did all he could to make up for lost time.

There was rarely an evening when they did not go out, and he would happily agree to Abbie's choice of entertainment—even when she hesitantly suggested that they might go to see a wrestling match.

Barbara, appalled, muttered stiffly about dignity, decency and what was fitting for a lady—to which Abigail replied stoutly that she was now a married woman and had already seen the best there was to see.

And so the wrestling matches at Jennyport's municipal hall became a regular Thursday night outing. Colin derived more amusement from his wife than from the contestants and would laugh as she bounced up and down on her front row seat, punching and catcalling, losing her hat and her hairpins.

When it was over he usually took her round to Uncle Sammy's to give the old man an account of the bout, and from there they progressed to Sammy's local, a waterfront pub named the 'Indian Clipper'.

Barbara said they were lowering themselves and that it reflected badly on her. She hoped that none of her friends found out, and hinted that Abbie was dragging her husband down most shamefully. She was appalled to learn that Colin actually liked the company at the Clipper, that he found those common boatmen to be amusing, admirable—and even wise. Barbara had always been aware of his tendency to scoff at the proprieties of his own class. If he had married her she would have corrected that. Instead, Abigail was making him worse.

Theirs was a companionable marriage, more dependent on humour than grand passion and probably healthier for being so. They began without illusions, ambitions or fanciful ideals and therefore suffered no clash with reality. Abbie had married a good friend in Colin Wylie and he brought her a sense of safety, of having a firm foothold in life. She now recalled her single years as cold and beset with uncertainty, although they had never seemed so at the time.

During the early months she would not have believed that anything could sweep away her contentment—and yet something eventually did.

The first sign of unrest appeared one evening at the music hall. Abbie sat happily through jugglers and acrobats, two sea shanties and a poem bemoaning the evils of alcohol. The next item, however, involved three young men dressed in baby clothes to perform a rather silly nursery scene.

Colin, aware of a sudden tension, glanced uneasily at his wife.

They had been married for nearly two years and still there were no children. He himself had no fears that anything might be wrong. He thought it simply a question of luck—hit or miss—and no one could accuse them of not trying. Abbie, however, was becoming restless. He had come home one day to find her poring over a pile of medical dictionaries and 'Home Doctor' books. She made some excuse about a sore throat but he had later found a page turned down at the section on 'barrenness'.

'Hey.' He nudged her. 'Stop brooding. You're making yourself miserable over nothing.'

'It isn't nothing. There's something wrong with me.'

'Rubbish. Look, they've finished. What's on next?'

'I don't know. Have a look.' She handed him the programme, having lost all interest in the show.

'Abbie, you're not yet twenty-two. My sister had three after she'd turned thirty.'

'She married late.'

'That's not the point. I'm saying that we have plenty of time.'

'Perhaps it isn't a question of time.'

'If you like we'll go home right now and have another try.'

Quietly she began to laugh. 'All right then. If you're feeling lucky.'

But they were not lucky and just over a month later a casual remark, innocently made, turned Abigail's doubts into real alarm.

It was nearly nine and the Clipper was packed with people; fishing folk, local traders, a few curious tourists looking for 'atmosphere', plus a selection of strange inebriates, all of whom lived within two hundred yards of the quayside.

Abbie and Colin arrived slightly earlier than usual to find Sammy sitting at a corner table with his neighbours, Bethany Wheeler and her husband Jamie.

They were very young, both under twenty. The boy was sturdy enough but his wife had a frail, undeveloped look about her and could easily have passed for fourteen.

'How was the wrestling tonight then?' Sammy twinkled at his niece, puffing contentedly at his pipe.

'Not so good as usual. You know—half-hearted.'

'She likes to see them carried out unconscious,' added Colin, winking at the Wheelers.

'You should take her to the ram-roast at Hallenhawke, lad. The local men do a spot of wrestling and it's not often there's one left standing at the end of it. No rules, see.'

'Hey, what about it, Colin? Shall we go?'

'When will it be?' he asked Sammy.

'First Saturday in October. I haven't been out there for years, mind you. Didn't want to run into Ivy, see. People come from all the surrounding villages for it. In the evening they have bonfires and a bit of dancing, plenty of cider and mead and sloe gin.'

'Sounds like quite an occasion. I didn't know anything ever happened in Hallenhawke. The place is like a graveyard for most of the year.'

'So it is, so it is. I reckon the ram-roast is the only bit of life they ever see—and they know how to make the most of it.'

'It's good fun,' said Bethany. 'We've been there several times and I can recommend it.'

'Will you be going this year?' asked

Abbie. 'We could pick you up and make it a foursome.'

'Well, no, we thought we'd give it a miss for once. 'Tis all a bit rowdy and tiring, what with Beth expecting in December. Doctor said she ought to take it easy, being small like she is.'

'Strange, isn't it,' added the girl, 'my older sister is far stronger than I am and yet she can't have children at all, poor thing. She's been to the doctor but he was no help. Don't think he knew what was wrong. And I mean to say, what's she going to do with her life if she's got no babies?'

'When you've got seven or eight of your own you'll be glad to share them with her ...'

Jamie's grin faltered as he noticed Abigail's expression. In confusion he glanced at his wife. She, too, was looking uncomfortable, for despair and annoyance were writ large on Wylie's face.

There followed an awkward silence and

Sammy tried to fill it with talk of fishing and laments about the new-fangled pleasure boats cruising up and down the coast. The Wheelers were unresponsive and Abigail wasn't listening at all.

'Do you want to go home?' whispered Colin.

She nodded and said to Sammy, 'I think we'll be going now. We didn't intend to stay out too late tonight.'

The old man winked at her. 'That's right, girl, that's sensible. 'Tis early nights that have kept me sprightly and youthful.'

They got up, wishing goodnight to the Wheelers, and made their way through the crowd.

'What's bothering Abigail?' enquired Jamie, feeling oddly guilty.

'We said something to upset them, didn't we?'

The old man tapped out his pipe. 'I could hazard a guess but I don't think she'd want us discussing it. Now then, will you have another drink, boy?'

Outside, a strong wind had sprung up and it was nearly high tide. Heavy waves cannoned into the old stone walls of the quay, hurling clouds of spray over the top as the Wylies made their way across the waterfront.

'Come away from the edge, you'll get soaked,' yelled Colin above the boom and hiss of the sea.

Abigail shrugged.

'Come on!' He pulled at her arm and she followed him across the street.

'Looks like they're expecting a rough night.' He indicated the houses on the quayside. Their shutters were already closed in readiness for a summer storm—as a shield against the hail of sand and stones flung up by the sea. 'We'd better go up to the square and get a cab.'

'I don't mind walking. I like heavy weather.'

'Well, I'm damned if I do.'

She stopped and turned to face him. He could barely see her features in the dusk.

The hair whipped and billowed around her face as the wind rose to a howl.

'Colin, if there's nothing wrong with us then why haven't we got any children? Why is it that a fragile little thing like Bethany Wheeler, who's only been married six months, is already expecting her first ...'

He pushed his hands into his trouser pockets and hunched his shoulders uncomfortably. 'I don't know, love, it's ...' He shook his head helplessly. 'I don't know.'

They walked on for a hundred yards or so, then she said, 'I think I'll go and see Dr Mackie. Maybe he can give us some advice.'

'Such as what?' responded Colin indignantly. 'As far as I know we've done everything that's necessary.'

'Oh, repeatedly,' chuckled Abbie. 'Don't think I'm complaining. You've been very diligent.'

'Quite,' he muttered, still faintly wounded.

'But that's precisely why I'm worried. You can understand that, can't you? At the rate we've been going we should have struck lucky by now.'

'All right. If it'll set your mind at rest then go and see Mackie. He'll probably recommend a large dose of patience.'

'I just hope it's that simple. I've got a horrible feeling that I may end up like Bethany's sister ... Oh! Colin, look. Out on Pelaze point.'

Far out on the skyline a light soared into the air, curved over and burned brightly for a few seconds, then went out. Half a minute passed and up went another flare.

'Oh, God, some poor soul's run on to those rocks. It's so dark out there I can't even see what sort of vessel it is.'

A heavy, gnarled man in high boots came pounding down the street towards them, struggling into his jacket as he ran. He hurried toward the Clipper to summon help and sometime later they saw seven or eight men in oilskins running for the boathouse.

By this time the sea was boiling and seething with a massive swell. From the surrounding cottages people began to appear, several dozen of them, to stand anxious and shivering by the harbour wall. Within a few minutes the lifeboat trundled down the slipway to hit the water with a mighty smack and hiss of spray. The people of Jennyport watched without speaking as the little boat ploughed out to sea. It reared across the top of a mounting wave, plunged down the other side and came up again, rolling. Finally it vanished into the darkness towards Pelaze.

The Wylies, like everyone else, were drenched and Colin pulled his wife away.

'There's no point in standing here. Come on, we'll get a cab.'

Reluctantly she trailed after him, still peering into the blackness over the bay.

It was August the ninth. She recalled it ever after as a day of gloom and misery that saw eight men drowned—four of them her friends—and her own descent into a ghastly depression which lasted for weeks.

Worry, once kindled, has a way of feeding on itself until all sense of proportion is lost. Somehow the fears stand out bolder than the reassurances and nothing the doctor said could remove the conviction that she was not going to get the family she wanted.

Colin found himself living with a preoccupied and melancholy woman who was rapidly losing her colour, her interest in life and a considerable amount of weight.

Barbara couldn't fail to notice that something was troubling her sister. She watched eagerly for signs of strife in the marriage and was mystified at their absence. Colin had not, to her knowledge, begun to stray. His career looked promising, for he was never short of clients. Abbie had plenty of money, plenty of outings. What more could she want?

The answer, though obvious, eluded Barbara for some time—perhaps because she herself detested children and would hardly have counted them among the good things of life.

Eventually, however, she began to suspect the reason for her sister's gloom and one day soon afterwards she tested Colin with vague questions about a family. His replies were evasive, suggesting that this was a troublesome subject he would rather avoid. Cautiously, Barbara pressed him further.

'Oh, but every man wants a son,' she said. 'Doesn't it bother you? Don't you feel cheated?'

She was disappointed to hear him say that he felt neither deprived nor worried and he certainly attached no blame to his wife. Children, he said, were less important to him than to Abigail and it was only her continued fretting which caused him real concern.

Barbara went away to consider and

digest this development, torn between hope and irritation. Abigail, she thought, was the most fortunate of women. Not only was she blessed with money and a highly desirable husband, but it seemed she might also be spared the gross inconvenience of child-raising.

There would be none of the discomfort and indignity of childbirth, with the subsequent ruin of one's figure, the midnight screeching and the annoyance of an ever-present, clinging infant into whom one was expected to shovel stewed fruit and then mop up at the other end. The whole shuddersome business had always disgusted Barbara. If Abigail did not appreciate her lucky escape, if instead she was fool enough to mope over it and place a strain on her marriage, then Barbara could see possible advantages for herself.

For the moment Wylie was obviously nonplussed and didn't know how to cope with Abigail's misery—but sooner or later, if she didn't pull herself together, he would begin to get tired of it, thought Barbara confidently. She was looking forward to that.

SEVEN

As it happened, Barbara's hopes were short-lived. Some weeks later events took a turn which was not to her liking, for Abigail found a way to soothe the anxiety.

She had almost lost the habit of visiting friends during the daytime. The sight of their offspring served only to upset her, as did the tactless questions and coy hints about 'some of your own, dear.' Worse still were the pitying looks of those who guessed what was wrong and made awkward efforts to cheer her up. Everyone appeared to be busily breeding and, unless she did likewise, Abbie felt she had nothing in common with them.

Lacking company and being of a leisured class, she found herself with nothing to do while Colin was at work. The old standbys of sewing and reading proved useless. The stitching was an almost mechanical process which failed to occupy her mind and the words of the latest novel were scanned but not absorbed as her thoughts ran their own course.

Finally, on a morning in mid-September when she had drifted into town for need of exercise, she found herself outside the window of *M. & J. Polliford, Furnishers and Suppliers of Household Linen.* They were having a sale.

Her gaze skimmed indifferently over the goods on offer—until it fell upon an item of furniture far back within the shop. She pressed her face close to the glass but failed to get a better view and so she went inside.

It was a desk. A beautiful mahogany desk, amply supplied with flaps, drawers and pigeon-holes to suit the fussiest clerk, the most orderly businessman. Colin would like it. He was untidy by nature, but perhaps with such a desk he would not keep losing things. It could only be an improvement on the ancient bureau in the study at Gypsy Hollow. Yes, it would be a fine present for him.

Abbie looked at the price and winced. The desk was clearly not a sale item, but—well, what did it matter? She was a rich woman and the prospect of surprising her husband brought back a breath of the old happiness. Anyway, money should be used to make life brighter and more comfortable—and if she was to have no children, then why should she save it?

Colin received the desk with such obvious pleasure that Abigail quite forgot her misery and was passably cheerful for a day or two afterwards. When at last her troubles began to seep upwards once more, she sought to submerge them in another burst of generosity. Barbara was puzzled and faintly embarrassed when presented with a large bottle of expensive cologne, but managed to thank her sister graciously enough.

Gradually, Abigail's trips into town became a daily routine. The buying became more diverse and impulsive, sometimes without regard to quality or necessity. The items, once acquired, ceased to hold her interest. All the pleasure lay in seeking out and buying things—and especially in giving them away to friends, relations and often the servants, too.

Each day she would return with her arms full of packages—ornaments, an electric iron, a new set of kitchen knives for the cook. On one occasion three oriental rugs were delivered. They were brightly patterned and not a room in the house seemed suitable for them.

Then there were the new clothes. She ordered dresses by the half dozen, with shoes to match. The dressmaker was delighted and Colin felt relieved that Abbie was at last taking pleasure in something after the weeks of despondency. He wondered briefly if she would ever manage to wear so many outfits, but if they made her happy ...

Barbara regarded the mounting pile of frippery with impatience. Of course Abbie would never wear all those clothes. Most of the outfits were tried on once or twice, then crammed into the wardrobe and forgotten. There were books, too, collected for their fine leather bindings but never read. From Billings and Walsh the cabinet makers came a bedroom suite in pink, with an elaborate scrollwork motif in red and gold. Barbara thought it looked cheap and disgusting. And worst of all, she decided, was the jewellery. Abigail would buy anything that was bright and flashy, defying every law of good taste.

'Just like a magpie,' observed Barbara sourly. 'She's got about half a dozen trinket boxes, all overflowing with the nasty, cheap stuff.'

In January the staff bedrooms were redecorated and everyone got an extra fifteen pounds a year. Parties were thrown with the most expensive food and wine that Jennyport could supply, and Barbara was appalled to learn that her sister had given the butcher's boy five pounds for his birthday.

Colin said it was just a phase and that it wouldn't last. He thought it was a comfort to her, that it took her mind off babies and that she would soon get bored, for money is no real novelty to the daughter of a wealthy man.

He was wrong. The buying went on and on until Barbara became thoroughly alarmed. Half of the money that Abbie was spending so wildly should have been hers and Barbara cursed her father for his foolishness. He had chosen to split the cash unfairly—and now it was being squandered.

What enraged her even further was Colin's refusal to take his wife in hand. He always sided with Abigail, even when she was clearly in the wrong. It seemed, after all, that he really didn't care about the money, that if it disappeared overnight he would still remain faithful to his wife. It was no longer possible for Barbara to delude herself that he had married Abbie purely for gain, and perhaps it was the awfulness of this that finally provoked her to murder her sister.

Abigail was feeling guilty. She had been on a two-day shopping trip to London and her latest purchase was still carefully hidden at the bottom of her case. For once, Abbie was in no great hurry to unpack and show her husband what she had bought. In fact she was very reluctant to mention it at all and thought it might be wisest to say she had purchased nothing in London. It would sound improbable, of course, but that was surely better than admitting she had spent a vast sum of money on a single item, lovely though it was.

It had looked so enticing, lying there on its black velvet cushion. And yes, one could argue that it was a good investment, for such a thing would undoubtedly increase its value in the course of time—but as an impulse buy it was still outrageous.

She had been delighted with her find until the time came to return home, and then doubts began to surface. Abbie knew that Colin wouldn't be angry, but he might think her a fool—and she didn't dare imagine what Barbara would say. That was why, in a fit of panic, she tore up the receipt, which of course served to make things even worse.

And so, when Colin asked about her trip, she shrugged and blandly said that the journey was enjoyable but the shopping had been disappointing and so she had spent most of her time sightseeing. Colin seemed pleased and Barbara was most surprised.

As for the guilty secret, it eventually took its place with the rest of Abbie's personal belongings. And within a few weeks, in her light and careless way, she almost forgot the importance of it. In the end, of course, she would doubtless have re-sold it, if she had lived long enough.

Another party. Another noisy, greedy gathering, chewing their way through Kendrick money, pouring it down their throats in vintage wine and Napoleon brandy.

Barbara had long ceased to look on these parties as pleasant social events. They were just another extravagance in Abbie's search for gaiety. Oh, the desperation was still there, but she had tamed it and there was no sign of strain on her marriage. The final irony, thought Barbara irritably, would be for Abbie to run through all the money in her panic—and then find herself pregnant after all.

On this particular evening Barbara was feeling unusually ill-tempered. Half of the people present were strangers to her and not of the type that she would invite home. Her gaze fell on a red-faced, pot-bellied man who was laughing and flirting with that ridiculous Jessie. They both had the same soft, porky appearance and Barbara thought viciously that Miss Redmond would look well on a platter with an apple in her mouth.

Colin, though, was enjoying himself immensely. He loved company and would chat tolerantly with the drunk and the boring as well as those he liked. Abigail was obviously tipsy. The drink made her clumsy and she caused some amusement by tripping over her own feet whilst waltzing with Chris Gilley.

To compound her annoyance, Barbara had spotted amongst the guests an old schoolmate, a blonde girl with the smiling eyes and the lazy manner of a contented cat. Her name was Hilary Borlase and she had spent the past four years in Paris.

Barbara's gaze slithered expertly over the girl's cream silk dress and recognized it as expensive and far ahead of local fashion. Hilary had certainly changed. The years in France had given her poise and wit. She chatted softly to the men in a smooth and confidential tone and they seemed enchanted. Barbara hoped that Hilary had not come home for good.

She became aware that Geoffrey, in his halting way, was asking her to dance. She refused him abruptly and pushed her way past a second young hopeful without even answering him. They were getting on her nerves, all of them.

'Barbara, dear,' said a voice beside her, 'whoever did your hair for you? Most unusual. Is it a new fashion? The ruffled look?'

The voice belonged to Hetty Ryder, who stood with two other smug-faced women by the fireplace.

Barbara put a hand to her hair and discovered several snarled, drooping curls and loose pins. She blushed angrily.

'How sweet of you to tell me.'

'It's a pleasure.'

She hurried upstairs to her bedroom and locked the door. It had been redecorated since Ivy's intrusion and was now pale pink. Every time she entered this room, Barbara was reminded of the humiliation at Abigail's wedding.

And wasn't Abbie looking a fright tonight? Barbara's mind fastened with loathing upon the image of her sister in that appalling green dress with all the cheap, twinkling jewellery. With so much money, could she not exercise a little more discrimination in her buying? Good jewellery would at least be a form of investment. To buy so much trash was like burning five pound notes. And of course it would just go on and on until there was nothing left, unless somebody stopped her ...

The idea, twisting like a worm below ground, was working its way to the surface. A thought half-acknowledged, never faced squarely. When it came too close to her consciousness she would veer away and think of other things. But it became daily more insistent with every new outrage, every new crop of needless bills. If only there was some safe and practical way to get rid of Abigail ...

Barbara had no real wish to return to the party and was tempted simply to get undressed and retire early. The clock said nine fifty-five. She sighed. Only another hour or so. She could bear that for the sake of appearances.

Carefully she repaired the hairdo, then softly opened the bedroom door and slipped outside.

Turning, she caught her breath, for there, farther along the landing and only a few paces from the staircase, stood Abigail. She was fumbling for something in her evening purse. Barbara stiffened, her grey, speckled eyes fixed balefully on her sister's back.

If it wasn't for you ... The thought dissolved into numerous little byways. Colin, the wedding, Roland's will.

She padded a few steps forward and stopped. Abbie was still unaware of her and yet it seemed to Barbara as if she was begging to be pushed. The malign fantasies suddenly became real and immediate. Downstairs, the door to the lounge was closed. No one would see. Just one little shove would be enough. Everyone knew Abbie had been drinking ...

For a moment she was afraid to move. Abbie would hear the rustle of her dress, would guess what was in her mind. If only there was time to consider and decide.

With a snap, Abigail closed her purse and started towards the stairs. One step down, another.

The opportunity was slipping away. Barbara suffered a single moment of indecision before instinct took over.

In all the months that followed she could never clearly recall her swift steps across the landing, just the feel of green satin against the palms of her hands and the solid warmth of the body beneath, the instant of pressure and the slight resistance as Abbie's fingers clutched at the banister, scrabbling and sliding on the polished wood. Committed now, and not daring to fail, Barbara tore loose her sister's grip and punched her knuckles into Abigail's back. There was a rattling gasp of fright as she lurched forward and then the dull, bony thud of the tumbling body.

The last thing Abbie saw clearly was the sunburst, the gold and copper pattern laid out in mosaic on the floor of the hallway. There for an instant it was spread out below like a great yellow flower and then her spine made sharp, bruising contact with the edge of the stair, once, twice. She was rolling, bouncing, and in that endless moment of falling there were flurried glimpses of carpet, banisters, wood panelling—and above her, drawing ever farther away, a girl in a pale blue taffeta dress.

Barbara. It's Barbara. Why did she ...?

Suddenly, something like a clamp closed around her neck and head. There was a brief wrench—and that was all.

To Barbara, watching white and breath-less, came the sound of a dull, tugging snap. Abigail's head had gone through the banisters so that the weight of her tumbling body had twisted and broken her neck. She lay at what seemed a bizarre, almost impossible angle, like something completely disjointed.

That was when Barbara fled.

She returned to her bedroom and sat shaking before the dressing table mirror while she swiftly unpinned her hair. Gradually her breathing began to steady, the heartbeats were slowing, the brilliant flush draining from her face. She picked up a hand mirror and pressed the cool, gilt backing to her cheek. Ten minutes passed.

Downstairs the music suddenly stopped. Dimly she heard raised voices and knew they had found her sister. Her eyes fixed unseeing on the hands clasped tightly in her lap as she listened and waited.

There were hurried footsteps, someone running up the stairs. Barbara reached for the hairbrush.

Someone rapped frantically at the door. With long, careful strokes she began to run the brush through her hair.

'Yes?'

The door opened and a small teenage maid peered in.

'Oh, Hazel. Are you any good with these things?' She gestured at the pile of hairpins and combs. 'Heather didn't do a very good job tonight and it's all come undone.'

The girl hovered in the doorway, her face a picture of fright.

'Well, come in then.' Barbara sounded impatient. 'Whatever's the matter with you? I'll show you what to do. It's just that I can't manage the back.'

'You'll have to come down, Miss.'

'How can I?' retorted Barbara testily, lifting a tress of hair and then letting it drop. 'They'll think I'm a wild woman.'

'I was sent, Miss, to fetch you.' Hazel began to cry.

'Oh, for heaven's sake ...'

'Mrs Wylie's had an accident.'

Barbara frowned. 'Accident?'

'I think she's dead,' stammered Hazel.

Was it good? Was it convincing? Did she look sufficiently shocked? Hazel, of course, was none too bright and therefore easy to fool.

'Oh, good God!' muttered Barbara.

Grabbing a ribbon, she hastily tied back the mass of hair and pushed past Hazel to face the large and more perceptive audience downstairs.

They were gathered in the hallway, an awkward, shuffling semicircle around the foot of the stairs, most of them watching in silence. A few glanced up when Barbara appeared on the landing. She detected no accusation in their faces, just shock and bewilderment. On hers they read anxiety but no one realized what lay behind it.

Below her, Sammy and Colin were crouched upon the stairs beside the body. She looked down at Wylie's blond head as he bent over his wife. Barbara had never seen him cry before, and again the old anger ripped through her. Abbie was gone. Good.

Barbara's common sense advised a careful blend of restraint and concern. No hysterics, not too much grief. Everyone knew that the Kendrick sisters weren't very close and it would be unwise to over-react. Shock, yes. But weeping and wailing? No.

She hurried down the stairs and knelt beside Sammy Spry.

'How did she come to fall? Did you see it?'

Dumbly, the old man shook his head.

She sighed. 'Oh God,' she said. 'Colin, I'm so sorry.'

He didn't seem to hear.

Barbara turned to the guests. 'Please, would you mind leaving? You can't help—although I'd be grateful if someone would fetch the doctor.'

'What the hell is the good of that?' muttered Colin.

'Oh, yes, yes. He'll have to come,'

answered Sammy.

Somebody volunteered to call Dr Mackie and the crowd began to disperse with murmurs of sympathy. A woman was crying and two of the men offered to carry Abigail upstairs. Wylie pushed them away.

'I suppose she tripped. Those damned skirts ...' began Sammy.

Barbara said nothing, but patted the back of his hand. 'Would you like to stay here tonight? I'll have the maids prepare a room for you.'

'No. Thank you, but no. I'll just wait until the doctor comes.'

He stayed for about an hour and then went home, declining Barbara's offer of a carriage. He said a walk in the night air might help to calm him, and it was strange that the sight of that old man trudging miserably down the drive brought Barbara an instant of real remorse.

She went inside and found Colin sitting on the stairs. Now that they were alone she felt oddly reluctant to go near him—perhaps because the strain of pretence was becoming too much. Colin himself evidently didn't want her company or that of anyone else.

Heather had sent the other servants to bed. She found it necessary to slap the unfortunate Hazel, for the girl's wailing was upsetting Mr Wylie even further. He wouldn't go to bed but she managed to coax him into the drawing room to sit before the fire.

Barbara stopped her in the hall as she went to fetch him some tea.

'Heather, do you think I should stay with him?'

'No, Miss, I don't. He's better left on his own. Besides, I'm afraid he'll be there all night. There'll be arrangements to make tomorrow, Miss, and I don't think he'll be fit to see to them. 'Tis likely they'll fall on you, so you'd best have a fair night's sleep. I'll be around if there's anything he needs.'

Barbara flinched at the idea of making funeral preparations. Such details underlined the awfulness of what she had done. And yet in a way it was fitting, she thought grimly. She had set out to dispose of her sister and was obliged to carry it through to the literal end.

'Of course. I'll do whatever is necessary. Good night, Heather.'

While undressing she wondered if sleep would come easily, if fear of God and haunting would arise when she lay alone in the dark.

But no. Quite the contrary. The nights of lying awake, fretting, stewing in jealousy, were over. There would be no more such nights. Her thoughts would be more happily occupied with the future now that Abigail was gone.

Barbara climbed into bed and slept soundly till morning.

EIGHT

It came as no surprise that Abbie had left her share of Gypsy Hollow to Colin. What did amaze Barbara was the fact that her sister had bequeathed her half of the stocks, as if Abbie had wanted to set things right between them. Pricklings of guilt assailed her for a day or two, but promptly vanished when she discovered just how little of the money was left—a mere three thousand, four hundred and twenty-six pounds, seventeen shillings and fourpence.

At first she thought the accountants had blundered but an inspection of their records revealed that Abigail had almost depleted her funds in just over seven months. They knew of no large donations to charity and she had certainly bought neither houses nor land. It was impossible to produce a precise figure, but Barbara judged that some ten to twelve thousand pounds were missing. The accountants said uncomfortably that Mrs Wylie had been steadily selling her securities for many months—against their advice, of course. She had been somewhat vague as to what she meant to do with the money.

Stunned as she was, Barbara recalled the need for caution. She was, after all, supposed to be in mourning and was therefore careful not to throw any tantrums. Colin was too absorbed with his grief to care about the money and Barbara thought it wise to affect a similar indifference.

And perhaps, after all, some of Abigail's purchases were not so cheap and shoddy. Maybe, amongst the heaps of artificial glitter and the army of ornaments, there was something of great value, something she could sell and so redeem her share of the cash. A sly notion possessed her that

Colin would be none the wiser if she kept his share, too. Indeed, it would serve him right for allowing his wife to spend so freely. If he was so careless in his attitude to money, Barbara thought it only sensible to take charge of that herself.

However, all this could only be conjecture until she found out what the object or objects might be. Neither the furniture, the parties nor the redecorating could account for such massive expenditure. She knew that Abbie had given Ivy Whickle a hundred pounds to leave her in peace—but that was small change by comparison.

Barbara at first dismissed the idea that Colin might know what his wife had bought, that he himself had a mind to keep it all. No, it was not in his nature to cheat other people.

She began her search one morning by sorting through Abbie's belongings and using her own judgement. There were pieces of jewellery so blatantly ill-made that she discounted them at once. Much the same could be said of certain vases, figurines and paintings. In the end she was left with a small collection of possibles—articles which required examination by an expert.

There was a gold bracelet set with red stones of some kind, also a number of porcelain figures which seemed to be of good quality, and a gold snuffbox with an enamelled inset on the lid depicting a water-mill. She also chose an antique clock, together with an assortment of brooches, necklets, a small watercolour painting and—the most exciting find—a collection of coins, neatly boxed and mounted.

Barbara thought this highly promising, for her sister had never shown any interest in such things and might simply have bought them as an investment.

Lastly she went through Abbie's wardrobe. She turned the garments inside out and sought for things sewn into their linings. She even examined the buttons for signs of value and peered inside each hat and shoe, but nothing came to light. Finally, her sharp eyes ranged along the top shelf but it contained only a pile of mousey-coloured hairpieces and some silk stockings.

Well, that, it seemed, was everything. She assembled the suspect articles on the bed in her room and began packing them carefully into a trunk. There was nowhere in Jennyport where she might have them valued—besides which it would not look well to be seen selling her sister's things. Barbara guessed also that whatever Abbie had bought was brought back from her London trip, and only in London would she find the special expertise of those who dealt in precious items.

The following day she left on the early morning train—for a change of scene, she said. She would be gone for five days, possibly a week. Just an excursion to refresh herself and blow away the gloom. No one thought it strange and the staff were pleased to get rid of her for a while.

Certainly nobody imagined that her trunk contained anything but clothes and Colin was too much sunk into misery to notice that things were missing.

Sitting alone in her compartment, Barbara's mind lingered on the coin collection and thought it the most hopeful item. Perhaps, after all, the money would come to her—and Colin, too.

Primrose Allington's husband had always been a trial to her. In fact she would go so far as to say he had ruined her life. And yet, in her own quarrelsome way, Primrose loved Ralph, irrational though it might be. She was never a quitter and could not bring herself to dismiss her marriage as a failure, if only because the mistake was so painful to face.

She came from Essex and had met him whilst on a trip to Southend with her sister. They had actually competed for his attention and Primrose now recalled with irony the day on which she had 'won'.

He proposed to her in a café over a cup of tepid tea and demonstrated his love with a flashy engagement ring. The seventeen-year-old Primrose, whose mother worked in a laundry and whose father was an underpaid clerk, was most impressed with this bauble. She assumed Ralph to be a person of some importance when he spoke of past 'projects' and 'ventures'.

This commercial jargon concealed a truth which was less appealing. Mr Allington was a thief, an indiscriminate, opportunist thief who dealt in anything that would bring in a few pounds. To his credit (in terms of expertise) he had some knowledge of antiques and the jewellery trade—enough to recognize a quality item, even if he was unable to put an accurate price on it. Instinctively he would pocket the thing first and worry about its value later.

They were married in London and moved into a small flat above a bookshop.

After seven months, no longer befuddled by novelty and young love, Primrose began to wonder why their income fluctuated as it did. At times he would bring home bottles of champagne and charming little presents for her. A few days later he would be 'overlooking' the rent and avoiding the landlord. Expensive outings were interspersed with days of bread and dripping when Primrose had no money for supplies. She would ask him for more housekeeping and he always promised to go to the bank. Sometimes he forgot and at others he came home with a pocketful of cash. After a while this pot luck existence began to wear her down.

There was no particular day on which she discovered the truth, no confession, no shocking revelation. Awareness grew in her, subtly at first and with mounting certainty, that Ralph's 'business dealings' were not straightforward. She pretended a wifely interest in his work and pressed him for details. He parried certain questions and tried to sidetrack her on others, but occasionally he blundered and admitted to little 'irregularities' of practice. Primrose said nothing but she guessed what it meant.

The day he came home and muttered about 'moving to the countryside, away from the grime', Primrose knew he was in real trouble. Within two months they had moved into an ancient, leaky cottage in the Pennines where nobody knew them. It was the first in a series of midnight hops that took them from Yorkshire to Exmoor to Norfolk and finally Hallenhawke.

'Their marriage was now in its twelfth year. Primrose had done her best to change his nefarious ways, with some little success, though whether this was due to her bullying or to the lack of criminal opportunity in small villages, is hard to say.

On days when she was feeling waspish there would be short, petulant quarrels. He knew she didn't trust him and he often felt like a small boy under the sour eyes of a governess.

In fact their feelings for each other were oddly ambivalent. Sometimes he saw her as a shrewish little spoilsport, always nagging, prying, accusing, and on these occasions fights would break out—rowdy, unbridled fights when Primrose would fly at him, pulling his hair and kicking at his ankle-bones. Ralph usually found it necessary to wrestle her on to the floor and sit on her till she calmed down. It was fortunate that they had no close neighbours to complain about the noise.

On another level he realized that her criticism was well-earned, for her married life had been lonely and unrewarding. He didn't know whether to admire her loyalty or think her a fool for staying with him, but in his better moments he would confess to a certain fondness for 'poor old Prim'—even if she were a holy terror at times.

Primrose, in truth, did not like the countryside at all and she loathed Hallenhawke in particular. The bleak grassland and the looming shadow of the carn had a depressing effect. And yet she thought it safer to live out of town, as if those few miles of road were enough to separate Ralph from the temptation and the law. She felt anonymous and protected by the very loneliness of the place, able to imagine that the crowds with their valuables didn't really exist.

Her days were totally consumed by work for she provided virtually all of their income. Ralph was qualified for nothing other than petty theft and she didn't trust him to take a job in town. She grew fruit and vegetables, kept a goat and a dozen chickens.

Three mornings a week were spent cleaning for Mrs Millston-Blight at the big house on the Jennyport road. It meant a walk of nearly a mile each way, whatever the weather. Fortunately,

Mrs Millston-Blight was a generous soul and paid very well. She also asked Primrose whether Mr Allington would care to do a spot of gardening now and again. With much grumbling he was induced to weed her flowerbeds and chop wood twice a week. He thought it beneath his dignity but Primrose was adamant because they needed the money.

Time and again she thought of leaving him and wondered why the prospect didn't seem more attractive. Perhaps it was a question of habit, or maybe it was because he had never been unfaithful to her. Primrose wouldn't tolerate that. She would lie for him, live in dreary villages with him, even visit him in prison if the worst befell—but another woman? Just let him try it.

After all the discomfort and anxiety she had suffered for Ralph, Primrose expected no less than total loyalty in return. And it must be said that he had so far behaved himself in that respect. Oh yes, there were sly glances at women now and again, but that was all. He never actually did anything about it. Of course, no one's record can remain perfect for ever ...

NINE

No one could understand why Barbara came back from her holiday in such an evil mood. They had no idea of the real reason for her journey and the disappointment she had suffered in London. None of the items she took with her proved to be of outstanding value. The whole lot fetched less than seventeen hundred which left about ten thousand pounds still missing. She began to wonder if Colin might, after all, know something about it.

Her desire to coax him into marriage became ever more urgent—doubly so because there were now matters of propriety to be considered. Once the shock of Abbie's death wore off, sympathizers would begin to remember that it wasn't quite decent for Mr Wylie to be sharing Gypsy

Hollow with his unattached sister-in-law. They would start to whisper, speculate, offer kindly little warnings ('For your own good, my dear'). Colin wouldn't care what they said—but Barbara would. No one admired a woman who was being 'used'. Her cronies would not require proof. Their murky imaginations were all they needed and indeed the day soon arrived when the first, sugary innuendos began to filter through.

It was Saturday and Jessie had suggested to Barbara that they might take a stroll in the afternoon.

On the eastern side of the town the battered old streets of the waterfront opened out on to a broad, smoothly paved promenade. Here were the two smart hotels, 'Rossmore House' and 'Laburnum Court', their front balconies overlooking the sands. Between these two rival establishments lay an extensive park which offered a boating lake, tennis courts, a children's playground and bandstand.

There was also a small pavilion known loosely as the tea house. Jessie wanted a strawberry ice and they spent half an hour there, watching the boats pottering around on the lake.

Barbara was still in mourning dress. She was unhappily aware that black, of all colours, suited her least. She could never consciously pinpoint the way it emphasized her frosty pride and the hard, pale stare, for she did not recognize these faults. She only knew that she looked less feminine in black and that did not please her. Jessie's stout form was encased in a suit of blue broadcloth. The skirt stretched roundly across her rump and the short jacket strained at its buttons. Barbara liked the blouse, though, and her gaze lingered enviously on Jessie's Merry Widow hat with its blue feathers. It would be several months before she herself could return to colourful clothing without inviting censure.

They left the tea house at just after three-thirty and headed toward the main gates. Almost all of Jennyport's population seemed to be at large that day, together with several charabanc-loads of trippers. Most of the women were dressed in light, summer fabrics, making Barbara feel conspicuous and uncomfortable in her drab clothes. The day had turned out exceptionally hot and she wished she had stayed at home.

'Let's go across there,' she said to Jessie, indicating a narrow, shady walkway on the left. 'We'll avoid the crowds and get out far more quickly.'

Unfortunately, their short-cut brought them face-to-face with two of Barbara's less cherished acquaintances. Her mouth pursed with annoyance as she saw Hetty Ryder and Belinda Pierce strolling towards her. There were no side avenues to offer escape and in any case they had already spotted her and were advancing with smirking curiosity.

Jessie's face lit up. 'Ooh, hello,' she squealed. 'Isn't it lucky we came this way or else we might have missed you!'

'Isn't it, though?' echoed Hetty.

'Lovely to see you,' added Belinda, her eyes flicking with amusement over Barbara's costume. 'On your way home?'

Barbara managed a stretched little smile. 'That's right.'

'Dear me, and it's not yet four o'clock!' exclaimed Hetty. 'Such a lovely day, too. Or do you find it too hot?'

'You should have brought a parasol,' said Belinda, twirling her own frilly yellow sunshade.

'I'm sure Barbara has far too much on her mind to worry about parasols,' reproved Hetty. 'Or any other little vanity, come to that. She's clearly been under a lot of strain.'

They both nodded and murmured with sweet sympathy.

Hetty had a limp, clammy look about her, as if she were made from white plasticine. Her eyes were colourless, the lashes sparse. She spoke in a querulous mew and had uncommonly large feet. Belinda was taller and more obviously healthy but a receding chin spoiled what might otherwise have been a nice face. In character they were both equally jealous—even of each other—and quite unable to conceal their spite.

'We've been out since one o'clock,' volunteered Jessie. 'We walked all the way into town.'

'Heavens, you must be awfully tired.'

'We are,' confirmed Barbara, giving Jessie a sly push, 'and it's time we went home.'

'I'm not in the least bit tired ...'

'Then you can do what you like,' snapped Barbara, 'but I've got a headache.'

'Oh, does that mean you won't be coming to Chris Gilley's party tonight?' enquired Hetty sadly. 'You don't seem to go out much at all these days. Whatever can it be that's keeping you at home?'

'I recently lost my sister, if you recall.'

'Oh, yes. Yes of course. We understand.

And I suppose Mr Wylie is still in mourning, too?'

'Very much so.'

'I'm sure you must be a great comfort to one another,' purred Hetty. 'I always think it's especially hard on a man who's just lost his wife.' Her eyes glistened and her tone was lewdly suggestive. 'You know, the loss of companionship and all the other—benefits—of marriage.'

'And of course you yourself have no one to console you,' agreed Belinda, 'being still unmarried.'

'At twenty-five.'

'It must be very difficult for you.'

'Everyone says so.'

'We can't think what you did to deserve so many troubles.'

'I trust there are no financial worries?' prodded Hetty hopefully. 'Abbie was a bit extravagant, wasn't she? Too generous, the poor dear. I suppose you and Mr Wylie will come to some—arrangement—regarding expenses?'

Barbara's stony eyes fastened on her dangerously and Hetty flinched.

'Mr Wylie and I each bear the weight of our grief separately and privately. The loss of a loved one is not a pain which responds to human sympathy so much as to time and personal fortitude.'

'I'm sure you're both being very brave,' murmured Belinda, smiling.

'As to my domestic arrangements, those are frankly none of your business and I think it ill-mannered of you to question me about money at such a time—or indeed at any time.'

Hetty and Belinda at last seemed embarrassed.

'Good day to you.' Barbara swept past them and Jessie scurried after her.

'It was awfully rude of them, wasn't it?' she puffed, trying to keep up with Barbara's brisk strides. 'But I don't think they meant any harm, you know. They're just nosey.'

'No harm?' Barbara stopped and stared

impatiently at her friend. 'Don't you realize what they were suggesting?'

Jessie slowly shook her head.

'Don't you understand anything? Oh, good grief!'

They walked on without speaking, for Barbara had some disagreeable facts to consider. She found herself entrapped in a very awkward situation, one to which she had given no thought when she pushed her sister down the stairs.

It was, of course, fortunate that everyone had accepted Abigail's fall as an accident. Even the nasty minds of such as Hetty and Belinda had not conceived of anything as extreme as murder. Nonetheless, Barbara had placed herself in a compromising position with her brother-in-law, and one from which there seemed no immediate prospect of escape.

Colin was still immersed in his grief, oblivious to the embarrassment she was suffering. He seemed interested in nothing and no one—not even Barbara herself—and she found that very annoying. It was time, she decided, to inform him of the rumours and find out where she stood. With any luck he would feel duty bound to make some sort of commitment.

'Colin,' she said one evening after dinner, 'there's something I think we should discuss. I haven't mentioned it before because I knew you were under a lot of strain, but now, well, it's been almost five months and ...'

'Barbara,' he said wearily, 'please get to the point.'

He had settled himself in Roland's old chair in the inglenook. He had lost weight and looked very young, sad and strikingly blond in the black suit and tie. Barbara seated herself opposite him. The firelight threw dancing shadows on their features so that neither could clearly gauge the other's expression.

'People are talking about us.'

'Oh?' he murmured, uninterested.

151

'Colin, they're spreading rumours, drawing some very vulgar conclusions.'

'We've given them no cause.'

'It's enough that we live together in this house.'

'Barbara, we own this house. It belongs to both of us and everybody knows that. There's no reason for them to assume that we live in each other's pockets.'

'It suits them to assume just that.'

He sighed and turned his gaze to the fire. 'Then it can't be helped, can it?'

Her tone began to sharpen with annoyance. 'That's all very well for you, but I have to be more discreet in my behaviour. A woman's reputation is of great importance to her and I'd like to know what you intend to do about it.'

'It's not for me to do anything. It's for them to mind their own business.'

'But they won't do that and I'll lose all my friends.'

Colin chuckled. 'You know, I've never understood why you value the opinions and respect of that foul-minded, moronic crew who please to call themselves "nice" people, with their calling cards and their garden parties and all the other trivia.'

Barbara's first instinct was to make some sharp observation on the kind of company he kept at the Indian Clipper, but she thought better of it.

'I'm not asking you to like them, Colin,' she muttered. 'I just want you to save me any further embarrassment.'

'How?' He regarded her frankly. 'Are you proposing that I should move out?'

'I, well ...' for a moment she floundered. Had he not taken her meaning at all? Or was he simply ignoring it? She really couldn't suggest outright that he should marry her, although she had come as close as she dared. No, that would be too undignified. Barbara felt a hot wave of confusion wash through her. 'I just thought you might have some bright idea,' she ended lamely.

'I've no intention of being driven out

of my home by gossip,' continued Wylie. 'Beside which, if you recall, I'm the one who pays most of the bills. I may add that I don't mind doing that. I have a profession and an income, whereas you do not. But just how long do you think you could manage if I wasn't here?'

'It sounds very much as if you're keeping me,' said Barbara stiffly, 'and that's just what they've been saying.'

'You know I didn't mean it that way. I'm simply being practical.'

'Perhaps I should move out?' ventured Barbara, praying he wouldn't agree.

'That would be very foolish. Believe me, your money wouldn't last long.'

At that, her mind turned to the missing portion of Abigail's fortune.

'Ah, yes. Money. Colin ...' She hesitated. 'Did you realize quite how much Abbie was spending? I mean, did she always show you the things she bought?'

'Sometimes. I never took that much notice. Why?'

Barbara decided that she might as well be honest on this point.

'I just wondered how she managed to run through so much in so short a time.'

'Barbara, the house is crammed with the stuff she bought. That's where the money went.'

'But it's cheap stuff, Colin. Haven't you ever tried to reckon it up? She couldn't possibly have frittered everything away.'

He shrugged. 'It was her own money. I didn't keep tabs on her. In the end I lost track of it all, but as long as she was happy it didn't bother me.'

He bent to toss a couple of logs on to the fire and rummaged with the poker for a while, shaking down the ash. Barbara eyed him thoughtfully and wondered if he were lying. His very lack of concern struck her as suspicious. It wasn't natural and she didn't accept that Abigail's death caused him more sorrow than the loss of over ten thousand pounds.

'In a few months,' he said, sitting back

and crossing his feet on the fender, 'they'll find something else to natter about. The worst thing we could do would be to deny the rumours or start making other arrangements. All you have to do is ignore them.'

Barbara looked dubious.

'And personally I like a woman who isn't fettered by propriety. That was why I loved Abbie so much. She didn't give a damn about such things.'

His green eyes fixed on her with what could have been amusement—or was it meant as a suggestion?

Was that what he wanted—that she be more like Abigail? The notion appalled her, but of course it was only a means to an end, a facade which could be promptly dropped just as soon as they were married. Barbara decided that anything was worth a try.

'Yes, she was very—easy-going. I sometimes envied her for it. And I suppose a bit of gossip would never have worried her.'

'Not in the least.'

'Well,' she forced a smile. 'I'll try and be a little less sensitive.'

'Good. And stop worrying. Everything will work out, given time.'

It was hard to say whether his last remark was meant as encouragement—but it was certainly not a rebuff. Barbara was far from satisfied with this non-committal response but she was prepared to give him a little more time, even if it meant enduring the gossip for some months to come. A less stubborn person might have given up at that point, thinking it simpler to look elsewhere for a husband, but Barbara was never one for backing down.

TEN

September the twelfth was the day of the regatta and a big bonus for the shopkeepers of Jennyport. Special coaches and excursion trains brought hoards of trippers, and every hawker in the district came, too, certain of a good day's trade. Countless yards of bunting looped and fluttered along the promenade. On the waterfront, barrow boys offered cockles and winkles, alongside of stalls that sold fruit, sweets, bottles of ginger pop, copies of 'John Bull' and 'Ally Sloper's Half Holiday'.

For those uninterested in the race there were other diversions; a pierrot troupe on the promenade, charmers, fortune-tellers and a one-man band.

Jennyport was enjoying a fine September but hats, caps and boaters were still the rule, despite the warm weather. Dresses and shirts stayed buttoned up to the neck and only the more venturesome were bold enough to hire a bathing machine and go in the water.

'What are you thinking about?'

'I was just watching the bathers.'

'I'm sure I don't know why they do it,' sniffed Barbara. 'Splashing around in ice cold water, wearing a silly suit, with everyone staring at them.'

'I suppose they enjoy it. Makes them feel sporty,' said Colin.

'It's undignified, that's for sure.'

'You're being prudish again. Anyway, I thought you liked being stared at. Why don't you try it yourself? You'll never have a bigger audience.'

Barbara ignored that. His flippancy had always annoyed her. She would set about curbing it as soon as they were married. In the meantime, however, she was obliged to show tolerance in order to achieve that. For the sake of her temper she sought to change the subject.

'Can you tell who's winning out there?'

'Haven't a clue. It all looks a bit aimless to me. Are you very interested?'

She shook her head. Barbara always found the sailing races boring, since it was difficult to distinguish either the outline of the course or who was in the lead. The rowing competitions in the evening could be quite entertaining, but they were many hours away.

'Then I suggest we go and look for somewhere to have lunch.'

'Oh, yes, let's,' she said, taking his arm. However, when they reached the end of the promenade and he kept on towards the waterfront, she began to fear that he was heading for the Indian Clipper. Barbara was doing her best to be genial but she didn't relish the idea of lunching on meat pies and ale in a common pub.

The tide was very low. On the sand beside the harbour wall a handful of people clustered around a gaunt, humourless character who was perched on the hull of an upturned boat. His name was Clem and he was a self-styled evangelist. Bank holidays and summer Sundays usually found him bawling sin and damnation in some public place, hurling strident scriptural quotations at his listeners while his wife played hymns upon a portable harmonium.

Glad of a diversion, Barbara stopped to watch.

'Don't tell me you've got religion?'

'Certainly not—at least, no more than anyone else. I just think he's quaint. Don't you find him amusing?'

'No. I'd call him six feet of holy misery.'

Barbara, in truth, had never found any joy in religion, for submission and self-sacrifice were not in her nature. In fact she found the whole business rather tiresome, but wouldn't dream of admitting it.

'We mustn't poke fun. He's a man of conscience.'

'How depressing.'

Clem's voice rose to an angry howl and

161

he pointed an accusing finger over the heads of his audience. They turned and saw that he had singled out a brightly dressed young woman walking along the quayside. The preacher began to bellow of harlots and corrupters of men. He drew comparisons with Athaliah and Salome, calling down judgement on all loose women and their consorts.

The girl stopped for a moment, scowling, tapping her foot, then she answered loudly.

'You'd know all about that, wouldn't you? And it seems to me you've had a lot more to say about trollops since Rosie Mingo overcharged you last Christmas Eve—specially as you were too drunk to get your pants down or your money's worth.'

The preacher's wife gasped and hit a series of wrong notes. Colin let out a roar of mirth and even Barbara sniggered, but her smile suddenly drooped and disappeared as she spotted Sammy Spry emerging from his cottage, not twenty yards away—for beside him trotted Ivy Whickle.

'Oh! There's Jessie!' She pointed vaguely towards a group of women walking in the opposite direction.

'Where? That's not Jessie ...'

'Oh, it is, it is. I must go and say hello. I'll see you later.'

She dived into the crowd and disappeared. It was only when he caught sight of Sammy and the old woman that Colin understood.

Ivy was sober and consequently sour, but her spirits seemed to lift when she saw Wylie.

'Ooh! It's Abbie's young man!'

She bounced up to him and slid her arm through his.

'Mrs Whickle. What a pleasure!'

Sammy nodded apologetically to him. 'Morning, Colin.'

'We're going to have our dinner at the Clipper,' said Ivy importantly. 'Aren't we, Sam?'

'We are,' sighed her brother.

'I bet you didn't expect to see me,' she went on. 'Nor did Sammy, come to that.'

'She turned up on my doorstep at eight o'clock this morning.'

'Didn't get much of a welcome either,' snapped Mrs Whickle. 'His own sister comes to visit him and all he can say is "God's truth, what do you want?" Looked at me like I was something gone septic.'

'I'm sure you're mistaken.'

'God knows, I don't bother him much. And I'm entitled to a day out now and again.'

'I expect he was simply shaken with delight.'

Sammy grinned and chewed on the stem of his pipe.

Ivy licked her fingertips and smoothed them coyly over her hair. Then she straightened her hat.

'Will you come and have dinner with us?'

'I'd be grateful,' added Sammy, for his sister had been cantankerous all morning and Colin's presence might serve to sweeten her temper.

'Certainly. But tell me—surely you didn't have to walk all the way from Hallenhawke? And how will you get home?'

'Walk? Oh no, I didn't have to walk. My neighbours brought me with them. Well, I say neighbours—really they live on the other side of the carn. Nice people though. Not like some of my relations.'

Sammy threw a glance heavenwards.

'You might know them,' continued Ivy. 'Mr and Mrs Allington?'

Colin regretted that he didn't know them.

'Pity. Quite good friends, we are. I often buy vegetables from Mrs A.'

'I see. And they have arranged to take you home?'

'Well, I suppose they will.' Ivy hesitated. 'Mind you, I never expected such great crowds. Might be difficult to find them among this lot.'

'If they don't turn up by four,' said Colin graciously, 'I'll take you myself.'

She wriggled with pleasure and her brother looked relieved. He didn't want a stranded Ivy left on his hands.

Only briefly, as they set off for the Clipper, did Colin pause to wonder where Barbara had gone.

Ralph had given Primrose the slip. For the past four hours she had clung suspiciously by his side and only when nature forced her to visit the public toilets in Jennyport Gardens did he manage to escape. After she had gone inside he hovered for half a minute, weighing a day's freedom against the scuffle that would follow when she caught up with him. It seemed like a fair bargain.

He darted across the rose garden, down to the main gates, and slipped in amongst the crowds on the promenade. From there he made his way up to the shopping centre and found it thronged with careless trippers, their pockets jingling. Paradise.

By half-past three he had acquired a shopping bag and a number of items to fill it. Constantly on the lookout for his wife and fresh opportunities, Ralph scanned the noisy crowds. That was when he noticed Barbara Kendrick emerging from a bookshop with a small, flat parcel in her hand.

Ralph doubted if she would remember him but he had certainly not forgotten her. She seemed to be alone and he thought it worth a cautious approach. Primrose would never know.

'Dare I hope that you remember me?'

Barbara frowned. She didn't like being accosted by strangers in the street.

'No, we haven't met before. And yes, you must be thinking of someone else.'

'Eggs?' suggested Ralph hopefully.

'What?'

'You bought some eggs from my wife.

Must be over three years ago, but ...'

'Good Lord, you can't expect me to remember that.'

'Maelan Carn, just outside of Hallenhawke.'

'Oh.' Barbara squirmed inwardly as she recalled the visit to Ivy Whickle. 'Oh, yes.'

'Ralph Allington.' He held out his hand and Barbara shook it limply.

'I'm Barbara Kendrick.'

'Is that Mrs, or Miss?'

'I am unmarried. And is your wife with you today?'

'Um, no. No, she has asthma and any excitement seems to provoke an attack.'

'Really?' Barbara sounded doubtful. 'She didn't seem the type. Too healthy, too energetic.'

'Oh, she's a gallant little lady—battles on, come what may.'

'Indeed.'

'Are you, uh, meeting someone or going anywhere special?'

'I'm on my way home, if you must know.'

'Then may I offer you a lift?'

Barbara hesitated. She didn't want to walk home, nor did she wish to go searching for Wylie—and possibly run into Ivy Whickle.

'That's very kind but are you sure it's convenient?'

'Perfectly.'

'Very well then.'

By the time they arrived at Gypsy Hollow, Ralph had learnt a good deal about Barbara whilst disclosing almost nothing about himself. He was very well aware that most people love to talk about their own lives and he used this fact to great effect, flattering her with admiring questions, marvelling at her answers. Barbara decided that he was, after all, a man of charm and intelligence. A bit pushy, perhaps, but much too amusing to give offence.

She paused on the front doorstep and

smiled at him awkwardly.

'I hope you'll understand if I don't ask you in. I am rather tired and no doubt your wife will be expecting you for dinner ...'

'Quite, quite.' Ralph concealed his disappointment beneath the broad, engaging smile. 'No apologies necessary. A chat with a lovely lady is reward enough.'

'However,' she went on, 'please feel free to call if you're passing this way again. I am often at home between four and six.'

'How very kind—and believe me, I shall take you up on it. Good afternoon, Miss Kendrick.'

In truth, Barbara dispensed this same invitation to almost all her male acquaintances—but it was no guarantee that she would actually receive them. Often, if she was feeling out of temper or otherwise engaged, they would be politely but firmly sent away, no matter how far they had come. It was her favourite show of power.

Ralph, however, was jubilant. He allowed

himself to fantasize on further, more intimate meetings, and became so lost in these imaginings that he was halfway to Hallenhawke before he remembered Primrose and, panic-stricken, bolted back into town to fetch her.

ELEVEN

Except for an all-purpose maid, Hilary Borlase lived alone. The death of her father and mother when she was sixteen had left her comfortable but not exactly rich. Freed from parental control, Hilary's personality had developed along very independent lines. She was neither prim nor cautious and, as impulsive girls are wont to do, Hilary embarked on an adventure as soon as she reached eighteen. She intended to see the world.

Well, ambitions tend to get modified along the way. There was not enough money for such an epic trip and she had to content herself with Europe. She spent two and a half years on the move, travelling through Italy, Switzerland, Holland and Norway—to name those countries which pleased her best.

Quite naturally she absorbed differing customs and attitudes. Noticing how widely they varied from one region to the next, she decided that correct behaviour was a pretty flexible concept and she might as well make her own rules. Those who are perpetually moving on need have no fear of what the neighbours will say and Hilary took full advantage of this.

She had several brief but energetic affairs with men who ranked from a wine waiter to the son of a rear-admiral. There were moonlight encounters on verandas, stealthy, barefoot creepings through hotel corridors at night, cryptic messages, grapplings in alpine chalets or under weeping willows by the river. All the things, in fact, that turn sex from a simple pleasure into an extravaganza. By the time she was twenty-one, Hilary Borlase had become quite a racy lady.

Finally, of course, she arrived in Paris and there became involved with a wealthy

173

restauranteur. Hilary and André went together like snails and garlic butter—so much so that their relationship lasted the better part of four years. Eventually, however, André took a fancy to a young widow from Rouen. Hilary, who was getting restless anyway, saw the way that things were going and elected to return home. They parted on good terms, but the end of a four-year friendship gave rise to some serious thoughts about the future. Now, in her mid-twenties, Hilary began to consider marriage and with this aim in mind she headed back to Jennyport.

She spent the next six months regretting it, for the lifestyle was unbearably tame and restricted when compared to her years on the Continent. A number of local women had united in the opinion that Hilary was a 'shocker' and they did not invite her to their homes. She dismissed the men as dull and despaired of finding another like André. They were all so proper, so boring—except one.

Hilary had always liked Abigail Kendrick and was genuinely sorry that she came to such an unhappy end. At the same time, however, she sensed in Colin Wylie a man who would suit her very well, if he could only be dragged out of seclusion. Respect and understanding had so far kept her from approaching him—but surely, after six months, it would be permissible just to ask him to dinner?

Content in the knowledge that Abbie wouldn't want her husband to steep himself in misery, Hilary resolved to pull him out of it in the simplest way possible. She was never one to waste time on coy manoeuvres.

And so an invitation arrived at Gypsy Hollow one Thursday morning—dinner for two at Hilary's home on Saturday night.

'Hazel, there's only one place setting for dinner.'
'Yes, Miss.'
'Aren't you going to tell me why?'

'Thought you knew, Miss. Mr Wylie's gone out.'

'Out? Where?'

'To dinner, Miss.'

'With whom?' Barbara's voice rose, indignantly.

'He mentioned a lady named Hilary, Miss.'

Barbara's stomach seemed to lurch. A certain unease had gripped her from the moment she spotted the Borlase girl at that ill-fated party. She knew with unfailing instinct that Colin would be sure to notice the fast and stylish blonde.

'Thank you, Hazel.'

She sat down and stared numbly at his vacant chair. The dining table, designed to seat ten, stretched away in front of her, vastly empty. Irritably, she picked at her meal, nibbling only a little from each course without enjoyment, conscious of the solitary clinking of her cutlery.

After dinner, Barbara complained of having slept badly the previous night and went to bed early, but she lay awake for several hours, fretting, planning and listening. It was shortly after midnight when Colin came in, obviously in good spirits. She heard him chatting and joking with Heather in the way he always did after a good night out.

There in the darkness, Barbara scowled to herself as she heard him trot upstairs to his room. Damn him, she thought. Damn him for being so wayward and so very difficult to control. Why could he not be pliable like the others? Once they were safely married she would make him sorry for putting her to so much trouble.

Of one thing Barbara was certain. If she had to compete with Hilary Borlase, she could not do it whilst wearing dowdy mourning dress. During the past months she had yearned for pretty clothes, for lace, frills and pastel colours. Black made her feel old and, what was worse, helpless. It gave Hilary an unfair advantage.

For all her style, no one could actually

call Hilary beautiful. Her face was too humorous, too feline. And yet, if Colin could bring himself to marry someone like Abigail, it would not pay to underestimate any woman.

Barbara knew she had a fight on her hands. And so, next morning, filled with determination, she went into town and spent fifty-five pounds on a new wardrobe. One could never do battle without the necessary equipment.

So it was that when Hilary called at Gypsy Hollow some days later, hoping to see Colin, she found Barbara decked out in pale green muslin, plus a choker necklet of small, amber beads. It was not entirely suitable for mid-morning, but Barbara's need for pretty colours was greater than her desire to be 'correct'.

'My,' said Hilary wickedly, 'you look as if you're going to a party—or have you just come home?'

Barbara didn't find that funny, nor did

she invite the other woman to sit down.

Hilary was wearing a skirt and jacket of chocolate brown velvet with a plain cream blouse. Her hat, of a similar brown and trimmed with a backward sweep of feathers, was slanted steeply atop the blonde hair. The contrast between the two women had never been more sharply underlined. Like grape and grain, they were best kept apart, but the desire for Colin Wylie had brought them face to face and the encounter was certain to be frosty.

'Is Mr Wylie not at home?'

Barbara's quiet laugh made it evident that she thought this a silly question.

'Why, of course not. It's Tuesday morning. Colin is at his office. He's a busy man,' she added significantly.

Hilary passed this off with a good-natured shrug. 'You must forgive me. I'm so used to mixing with the idle rich. One gets into bad habits.'

'I'm sure. Whatever made you come back to Jennyport? You're so obviously suited to a free and easy lifestyle.'

'Ah, but I always planned on marrying an Englishman. Continentals, you see, tend to be entertaining—but fickle.'

'It sounds as if you've had an unfortunate experience.'

'Yes, but it hasn't been wasted. I do believe that life is a learning process and the most valuable lessons are knowing when to quit and making sure one doesn't repeat one's mistakes. I never waste time on lost causes.'

In all fairness to Hilary, these remarks were made in reference to her own defunct affair with André and were certainly not aimed at Barbara. However, assuming as she always did, that the attention of the world was focused upon her, Barbara took them personally.

'I wouldn't know about that,' she answered coldly. 'I have never been cast off by a man.'

'Indeed,' murmured Hilary with eyebrows raised, 'it's a rare wench who's never suffered a disappointment.'

'And I think it degrading for a woman to actively pursue a gentleman.'

Hilary took her meaning at once but showed only faint surprise and not a trace of annoyance.

'Maidenly restraint is a commendable thing,' she said with a broad smile, 'but it's apt to get you nowhere.'

Thus far, neither woman had scowled or raised her voice and yet tension was growing with every passing second. Hilary had not expected such a hostile reception, but she was rapidly sizing up the situation and quite prepared to fight if necessary.

'What a lovely old house this is,' continued the blonde girl calmly. 'I do wish I lived here.'

Barbara quivered slightly but said nothing.

'André always said that if one wants a thing badly enough, one may eventually get it. Of course, if two people want the same thing, then it becomes a race, doesn't it? Tell me, are you competitive by nature?'

'I can always meet a challenge.'

'Pistols at dawn, eh?'

'Nothing so vulgar. Friendly rivalry,' corrected Barbara.

'Hmm. Well, I'd best be off now. It's been very interesting, Barbara. I always enjoy a good chat and I seem to have learned a great deal about you. Would you please tell Colin that I called?'

'I'll try and remember.'

'Thank you. He seems to be recovering from Abbie's death, don't you think? More like his old self.'

'Not at all. He's still extremely upset. He becomes very quiet and withdrawn here during the evenings—which is understandable.'

'Heavens, I am surprised. He was so very bright and cheerful when he came to dinner last week. I shall have to get him out and about more, shan't I? Pull him out of it, so to speak.'

'What he needs is peace and quiet, time to get over his loss. I allow him privacy and never bother him with social trivia. That is always the best way.'

Hilary's smile was taut and defiant. 'I'm sorry but I don't agree. Good day.'

Ralph had been in the doghouse ever since regatta day. Primrose hadn't cooked him a hot meal for three weeks. She wouldn't sleep with him either. A bunch of roses, stolen from Mrs Millston-Blight's garden, failed to appease her and his apologies were met with snorting cynicism.

He found her in the wash-house one Monday morning, sweating as she heaved a pair of sheets out of the copper. As usual there was water all over the floor and her hair clung damply round her face in the steamy air. He padded up behind her and smacked her playfully on the rump.

'Don't!' snapped Primrose. 'Idiot!'

Her face was red, puffy with heat and exertion.

'Oh, Primrose, darling ...'

'Go away. I'm busy.'

Ralph still hovered.

She hurled an armful of shirts and socks into the copper, poked them down into the suds with a wooden stick and slammed the lid on. There were several tin baths full of cold water on the floor, in which she was rinsing towels and tablecloths. She seized a couple of these items and thrust them between the rollers of the mangle.

'Oh, here, make yourself useful. Put those through.'

'Who, me?'

'Yes, you. Go on.'

Reluctantly he began cranking the handle and the rollers turned stiffly.

'Hard work, isn't it?' said Primrose acidly. 'Just wait until you come to do the sheets. By all that's natural, I should have muscles like a ditch digger.'

'You only have to ask, dear. I'd be happy to help you with anything strenuous.'

'The only worthwhile help you could give me would be to find yourself a decent job with a regular wage so that we could afford a servant to take on some of the work. One would be enough. I'm not asking for a life of leisure. But you can't be trusted to do that, can you? The old instincts are just too strong.'

'Why don't you let me try? First you complain because I haven't got a real job and in the same breath you're finding reasons why I shouldn't take one.'

'Past experience. I don't want to have to move house again. I couldn't face it.'

'Primrose, I promise you ...'

'Oh, yes, brim-full of good intentions. The fact remains that you've never in your life had a position where you didn't find some way of robbing your employer. I know where those roses came from, my sweet. I also know that Mrs Millston's cook won't allow you in her kitchen any more since she missed a whole salmon from the larder.'

'I try, Primrose, I honestly do. It's just that when I see things lying about ...'

'You can't keep your damned hands

off. You're like a child, Ralph. No responsibility, no self-control. Sooner or later people always get wise to you—like the cook—and we have to move again before you land yourself in real trouble. By God, you've had some close calls!'

She handed him a tablecloth. He snatched it away and flung it against the wall, where it hit with a wet smack and flopped to the floor.

'You see yourself as a kind of saviour, don't you?' Ralph's face was darkening with temper. His hair and moustache, plastered down in the heat, looked thin, sticky and mean. 'Poor long-suffering Primrose, the only thing that's keeping Ralph out of prison. Believe me, you're worse than any gaoler.'

'Then all I can say is you've got the fanciest cell in creation. I break my back to keep this house clean and comfortable for you.'

'Well, why don't you leave me, eh? If it's all so arduous, so unrewarding? I won't stop you and I won't come after you.'

'A wife has a duty to her husband ...'

'I can't stand it when you're being noble.'

'... no matter how weak and pathetic he is.'

'You are a nagging bitch, Primrose. And what kind of a life am I having, eh? Do you ever stop to think about that? Stuck here in this windy, God-forsaken place ... I'm a city man, Primrose. I do not like the country. I'll go further—I loathe it. But I agreed to live here because it was what you wanted.'

'Only to keep you out of harm's way,' she snapped. 'I can think of twenty places I'd rather be.'

'In that case I suggest you pack up your virtue and your martyrdom and move out. Go anywhere you please.'

'Two thirds of this house were paid for with money that I earned,' hissed Primrose, 'and I'm damned if I'll walk off and leave it for you.'

'Primrose, you don't honestly believe that living out here makes any real difference? For years you've been fondly telling yourself that I can't get into trouble as long as we stay out of town. For God's sake, woman, be realistic. You can't really think that a few miles of road would stop me if I wanted to go?'

She sat down on a footstool beside the copper. 'I don't know what else to do,' she said wearily. 'I can't tie you up and lock you in the cellar, and it seems I can't change you.'

'That is correct. You can't change me so why don't you make life easier for both of us and stop trying?'

'All right then. Damn well go and do what you please. There'll be no supper ...'

'That's nothing new.'

'... and no clean clothes, because this lot can stay where it is until it rots ...' Primrose kicked over one of the tin baths.

'I'll walk around naked if need be.'

'... and I will never, ever sleep with you again.'

'Fine. You can go on strike if it makes you feel better.'

'Get out,' she screamed, hurling the copper-stick at him. 'Go and enjoy yourself. Go thieving, get arrested. Get bloody well hung if the fancy takes you.'

'That might be a happy release.'

She buried her face in her hands and heard the door slam behind him. From the overturned bath a puddle of water was creeping round her feet. Primrose got up to fetch a mop and began blotting up the mess, still shaking with despair and anger. Despair because she knew he really couldn't help himself, anger because she would never understand why. All he had to do was stop thieving. Why should that be so difficult?

'Damn you, Ralph,' she muttered. 'One day you'll do something that will ruin us both.'

'Is Miss Kendrick at home?'

'I'll have to find out, sir. What name is it, please?'

'Mr Allington.'

Hazel returned some minutes later. 'Please come in, sir. Follow me.'

She showed him into the drawing room. Ralph had expected to see Barbara alone and was faintly annoyed to find her brother-in-law there also. Colin put down his newspaper and got up to shake hands with the man, but the look on his face was less than welcoming. He seldom disliked anyone at all, much less on a moment's acquaintance, but something about Allington aroused immediate distrust.

Barbara saw and misread his reaction. A tremor of excitement ran through her.

'Mr Allington was kind enough to drive me home from the regatta, Colin.'

'Oh?'

'We had met before, of course.'

'Only briefly, I regret to say,' added Ralph.

Wylie sat back and lit a cigar. 'Do you live locally? I have a good memory for faces but I don't recall yours.'

'No, I'm a country dweller. Out towards Hallenhawke.'

'Ah.' Something connected in Colin's memory. 'Would you be the same Mr Allington who drove Mrs Ivy Whickle to the regatta?'

Barbara almost jumped with alarm.

'So you know the, uh, lady?' said Ralph surprised. 'She sometimes buys fruit and vegetables from my wife and therefore considers herself a friend of ours.' Catching sight of Barbara's expression, he added hastily, 'Naturally we don't encourage her and I didn't actually offer her a lift. When I left the house after breakfast that morning I found Mrs Whickle already waiting in the gig. I think it would have been very difficult to dislodge her. She takes a lot for granted, I'm afraid.'

Barbara was visibly relieved.

'Hmm,' murmured Wylie coolly. 'So you're a married man, Mr Allington?'

'Well—yes, but,' he paused sadly, 'my wife left me just over a week ago and I've not heard from her since. I don't wish to be indelicate but I suspect she's been—you know—meeting someone. It was a very sudden, unexpected blow.'

'Oh dear, dear,' soothed Barbara. 'You must be terribly distressed—and lonely, too.' She peeped slyly at Colin, who was watching the other man without any sign of sympathy.

'And now you are seeking fresh female company with which to fill the gap and deaden the pain?'

Barbara's mouth popped open at Wylie's uncustomary rudeness and Ralph regarded him warily.

'As a rule I try to immerse myself in my work. It's the surest way to keep one's mind off personal upsets.'

'And what kind of work is it that you

find so therapeutic?'

Ralph had always been a quick and inventive liar.

'I'm a botanist,' he said, recalling some floral wisdom he had picked up from Mrs Millston-Blight's gardener. 'The various types of moorland in the Hallenhawke area provide a great many interesting species for study. Mosses and lichens on the carn itself, sundews and cotton grasses in the marshy areas, heath bedstraw, woodsage—the list is endless.'

'My, how clever you are,' cooed Barbara. 'Will you stay for dinner?'

'That would be delightful.'

Colin didn't look at all pleased.

It was nearly ten when Allington went home, feeling that he had made considerable progress with Miss Kendrick. Ralph hadn't had a woman for weeks, since Primrose had withdrawn her favours, and the idea of bedding a succulent, classy creature like Barbara put fire in his loins and a spring in his step. He would have been less pleased with himself had he known that she saw him as just another admirer—but one who could be used to make Wylie jealous.

'What a charming man,' she said to Colin. 'One so rarely meets a gentleman of intelligence and maturity.'

'I don't like him.'

She feigned surprise. 'Why ever not? I found him most amusing.'

'I don't trust him.'

'In what way?'

'In any way. I don't often jump to conclusions about strangers but he strikes me as sly.'

'Oh, Colin, really! I don't know where you get these ideas.'

'Don't encourage him, Barbara. He's not the type of person with whom you should get involved.'

She turned away from him, casually rearranging the bowl of roses on the drawing room table.

'We'll have to see about that, won't we?

I think you're being far too suspicious and over-protective. It's very kind, of course, but you mustn't worry about me.'

'May I remind you that he's married?'

Barbara ran her fingers lightly over the rose petals.

'But she's left him.'

'Yes, and you'd do well to ask yourself why.'

'Colin, please don't fuss.' She turned around and smiled at him. 'I'm surprised at you. You used to be so liberal and yet here you are telling me that Mr Allington is not respectable.'

'I wanted you to be tolerant, Barbara, not naïve, not reckless.'

Barbara glowed with pleasure. She herself saw nothing questionable about Ralph Allington and regarded Colin's dislike of the man as jealousy, plain and simple. It was unlike him to be possessive and she counted this as a small victory over Hilary Borlase. Perhaps Allington would be a handy weapon for the cause.

'Well if you really think he's not a suitable person to know ...'

'I do.'

'... I'll take care never to invite him to Gypsy Hollow while you're at home. That way you won't have to see him.'

'That's not what I meant! I think you should avoid him altogether. If he calls here again, don't ask him in.'

'I couldn't possibly be so rude.'

'Barbara, I don't want you to see him.'

'If you were in a position to forbid it then I would, of course, defer to your wishes, but I must remind you that I'm an independent woman, entitled to make my own decisions.' She was tempted to add, 'Unless you are offering to change that.'

Wylie's face was thunderous. 'Oh, all right. I'll mind my own business. Have it your own way.' He slumped down in a chair and disappeared once more behind his newspaper.

I'm sure I will—eventually, she thought.

Thereafter, Ralph was asked to dinner

at least once a week. His meetings with Barbara became more and more frequent, but he never invited her back to his home—where she would doubtless encounter Primrose. Barbara herself had no wish to go anywhere near Hallenhawke and was thus unaware that Ralph's wife was still firmly in residence.

Wylie was plainly annoyed at the relationship—which gave Barbara great satisfaction and convinced her that she was winning. However, some months later in April of nineteen hundred and ten, open conflict arose over a certain embarrassing incident and Barbara abandoned all caution in her dealings with Ralph. It was the worst mistake she ever made.

TWELVE

Somehow they didn't quite match. Barbara frowned at the doe-skin gloves. They didn't blend with the colour of her new coat. There was a definite clash and that would never do. Irritably she pulled them off and searched for something more suitable. That was when she remembered Abigail's tan suede gloves, bought shortly before her death, barely worn. They would serve nicely.

It was almost three-fifteen and she had promised to meet Jessie at half-past. Hurriedly she trotted up the stairs to the Wylies' bedroom and walked straight in.

In moments of confusion one sometimes notices odd little details. Good grief, he's got freckles all over his back! she thought. Her next reactions were shock to find him there at all, and fury when the woman beneath him peered over his shoulder and remarked casually, 'Oh dear, we forgot to lock the door.'

'Eh?' Colin rolled over and grabbed at the covers. 'What the hell are you doing here?'

'I, I didn't know ...'

'Well, what do you want?' His tone was even but the green eyes glared angrily at her.

Hilary sat up beside him and reached for the glass of cognac on her bedside table.

'To borrow some gloves. Abbie's suede ones,' Barbara said stiffly.

'They're in the third drawer.' He gestured impatiently towards the dressing table. 'And from now on I'd be obliged if you would knock before entering this room.'

Barbara's gaze flicked from her brother-in-law to Hilary's round and smiling face.

'It's the middle of the afternoon,' she said angrily. 'I hardly expected to find such a scene as this. I thought you were out.'

'One should never take anything for granted,' purred Hilary, sipping contentedly at her brandy.

'Is that a sample of Continental wisdom? You'll find your cheap Parisian behaviour is not tolerated here.'

'Do I detect moral outrage, or is it something else?'

'You are vulgar. You don't even have the decency to show embarrassment.'

'That's enough, Barbara.'

'It's all right.' Hilary put down the brandy glass and slid her hand across his neck and shoulders. 'Barbara's had something of a shock. We must make allowances. Why don't you try it yourself, my dear? I'm sure it would do you a world of good. I mean, look at me—happy, healthy, good-tempered ...'

'And coarse,' finished Barbara.

'The things we regret most are always the things we didn't do,' quoted Hilary thoughtfully. 'And how the years slip away.

No doubt you've noticed that.'

'I would rather be an old maid than engage in this sort of liaison.'

'That is becoming a distinct possibility. How old are you now? Twenty-six? Tell me, Barbara, why have you never married? I'm sure it's not for lack of offers. Or have you set your sights on someone unattainable?' The blonde girl's eyes sparkled with amusement.

'I shall marry when I'm good and ready. And unlike you I've done nothing to tarnish my reputation. Men seldom marry a woman who's been used.'

'Nobody is being used,' said Colin sharply.

'No, indeed,' murmured Hilary, snuggling up to him.

'If you want the gloves,' he said to Barbara, 'take them and go.'

'Thank you, but I can do without.'

'As you please.'

She was turning to leave when Hilary spoke again.

'One last thing—bad reputations don't always have to be earned. I'm sure you're aware that people are talking simply because you and Colin share this house. Personally I think it tragic to be falsely accused and if I couldn't stop the talk then I'd feel inclined to make sure I deserved it.'

Barbara left without answering.

'Did you have to?' sighed Colin.

'What?'

'Tease her like that. You know what a prude she is.'

Hilary bubbled with laughter. 'No, no. You're quite wrong. I don't think you understand Barbara very well.'

'Meaning?'

'That she would dearly love to be here in my place, but she also wants to keep her facade of upright, moral decency. Barbara is very concerned with appearances, Colin, but I'd bet half my worldly wealth that she's had some very lustful thoughts about you.'

'You can't be serious.'

'Oh, but I am. And I'll tell you something else. The only reason she puts up with the rumours is that she's planning to hook you. Then the gossip won't matter.'

'I couldn't marry her,' he said, aghast. 'I don't like her. Well, that is, I don't dislike her, but she's the last person I'd marry. We would never get on.'

'I don't think Barbara sees it that way.'

'Good God!' He lay down and pulled Hilary against him. 'What am I going to do?'

'Be direct. Tell her that it's not on. She'll probably throw a fit but it will be kinder in the long run, because sooner or later all those other men will get tired of waiting for her.'

He shook his head. 'Kind or not, it will certainly be unpleasant. Barbara takes offence very easily and I'm afraid it'll need more tact than I can muster.'

'All the same, I wouldn't leave it too

long if I was you. Get it over with quickly.'

'Well, maybe I'll see about it after we come back.'

Hilary perked up at that. 'Where from? What are you talking about?'

'I thought you might like a nice weekend in the country.'

'Oh, yes! I'd be so glad to get away from Jennyport for a while.'

'Then we'll get the evening train next Friday. Agreed?'

'Certainly.'

Barbara spent the next few days thinking up counter-attacks, but every idea—short of killing Hilary—seemed both inadequate and futile. She was still smarting helplessly from the encounter in Colin's bedroom when he announced, on the Wednesday, that he and Miss Borlase would be spending the weekend in Devon. Barbara received the news with a shrug and very little comment, but in truth it was more than she could stand.

As Hilary had so rightly said, if one was the victim of gossip one might as well deserve it. Indeed, she thought, the only effective way to hit back was to follow Hilary's example and spend a couple of days with Ralph Allington. She couldn't think of anything more safely guaranteed to annoy Colin.

It was just after five on Friday evening when he came downstairs with a small suitcase and popped his head round the drawing room door to say goodbye to her. She was sitting in the inglenook, placidly working on a piece of needlepoint.

'I'm off now. Should be back by lunch on Monday.'

'Have a good journey,' she said pleasantly.

'Hope you won't be too bored here by yourself.'

'Good heavens, no! Someone is coming to stay and keep me entertained.'

'Jessie, you mean?'

'Ralph.'

Colin's smile vanished. He stepped inside and closed the door behind him.

'Barbara, don't be a fool.'

She raised an eyebrow. 'I think that's a little strong, don't you?'

'The man is devious, he's ...'

'What? Exactly what do you have against him? He's never done either of us any harm.'

'Not yet. Look, Barbara, this house is my home, too, and you've invited him here in my absence. I don't like it. You could have asked or at least told me in advance.'

'Why?' flashed Barbara. 'You didn't see fit to inform me before bringing madam home to share your bed. It appears that you are allowed to have "friends" whereas I am not.'

'Are you doing this just to spite me?'

'Don't be ridiculous.'

He was silent for a moment, then he shook his head and opened the door. 'You stupid woman.'

Barbara gasped and turned to say something biting in return, but he had already gone.

I suppose it wasn't bad, if one overlooks the indignity. Not at all unpleasant but hardly a glittering experience either. All a bit twitchy and frantic. I wish I had more knowledge of these matters, then I could more easily form an opinion. At a guess I'd say he's competent but unexceptional.

Barbara sat propped against her pillows, a blue lacy bedjacket thrown across her shoulders. Beside her lay the inert figure of Ralph Allington. She cocked her head to one side and surveyed him with detachment. There was, she fancied, a collapsed look about him that spoke of total exhaustion. The peppery crop of stubble on his chin was most unattractive—but at least he was slim and well proportioned. Barbara hated flab.

Now that it was done, she found herself strangely unmoved by it all. There was certainly no shame or embarrassment, no feeling of having betrayed her honour. Delicacy, like face paint, was only for show. She felt instead a cool amazement that this activity should engender so much fuss. As for Colin, she realized with regret that he would never again inspire the same fanciful lust. She allowed that he might be far more expert than Ralph but much of the male mystique was gone for ever.

Not that she intended to give up. Getting her own way was a matter of principle. It was not in Barbara's nature to admit defeat, especially when the campaign had cost her so much. She had killed her sister to get him, she had patiently borne the gossip and done her best to be agreeable, much as it went against the grain. Lastly, she still believed that he knew something about the missing money and was damned if she would let some other woman get the benefit of that.

From her window she could see a single star, its light clear and sharp against the smoky wisps of dawn appearing in the east. She sat there for half an hour watching the night disperse as a grey morning filtered through. It was Sunday.

At last she got up, opened the door a fraction and peeped outside. The landing was deserted but the staff would soon be starting work. She slipped out, closing the door softly behind her, and padded back to her own room.

Hazel would bring her breakfast in bed at eight and Barbara would then get ready for morning service at ten. She always went to church on Sundays. It was doubly important to be seen there when one's reputation was otherwise in question—besides which, if she did not attend, then the Hetty Ryder faction would assume she had nothing new to wear.

Hazel took a tray up to Ralph at nine and found him semi-conscious. The smell of breakfast brought him round.

'Good Lord! Breakfast in bed! Very kind.'

'They always do this, sir, on a Sunday. Sort of a custom. Miss Barbara had hers an hour ago.'

'Did she now? How spartan of her. Never been an early riser myself.'

'She goes to church, you see. Ten o'clock service.'

'Ah, yes, naturally.'

'Will you be going, too, sir?'

He lifted the lid off the largest dish and found devilled kidneys, bacon and sausages.

'Mmph. Marvellous. Sorry, my dear, church did you say?'

'Yes, sir.'

'Ah, no. I think not. Don't feel too well today, actually. Back trouble, you know. I'll just stay here and potter about—read a book or something.'

He ate his meal in fine high spirits. Not only had he enjoyed a romp with the beauteous Barbara, followed by a sumptuous breakfast in bed, but he would also have the opportunity to explore the house while she was out.

There was a small basket of fruit on the tray. He selected a ripe pear and savoured it, considering the decor of this very comfortable bedroom. Sage green and white, the best of taste. This was the way to live.

By contrast, his own home was shabby and unwelcoming. He thought about Primrose with her drab, mended clothes, the straight black hair with never a ribbon or ringlet, and her constant bad temper. It couldn't be helped, of course. Their circumstances were not as he would have wished. All the same, he couldn't help but compare, and if only Primrose hadn't been so nervous and restrictive he might very well have become a rich man and owned just such a house as this. Yes indeed, if the truth be told, his wife did not appreciate him. In fact, she had stifled his talents with her tedious notions about honesty.

By ten-fifteen the house was very quiet. Heather and Hazel had gone to church, so only the cook and scullery maid remained to prepare the lunch. He recognized the need for caution, aware that Colin had no liking for him and might be quick with an accusation if anything went missing. Nonetheless, it wouldn't hurt to look around.

A swift tour of the house proved very interesting. The temptations were many and it pained him to resist. Had it not been for Wylie's obvious distrust and antagonism, he would have had a record haul. Enticing though it was, Ralph was afraid to take the risk. Primrose, he thought wryly, would have been proud of him.

By eleven-thirty only Colin's room remained. He was surprised to find it strewn with a woman's belongings and then realized that they must have been those of his late wife. By the look of them she was sadly lacking in taste. Even the clothes in her wardrobe were cluttered with frills and flounces, the colours unsubtle. He was about to close the door when something in the corner of the top shelf caught his eye. Something brown and furry.

For one startled moment he thought it was a small dead animal—but further investigation revealed a wad of false hair. Ralph was intrigued with this bit of female artifice, for Primrose never wore such things.

It was knotted and tangled, virtually inside out, and he guessed that its owner must have pulled it off in a hurry and tossed it to the back of the wardrobe—too tired perhaps, to run a brush through it. Too tired also to remove the beautifully made golden comb which was hopelessly snarled amongst the curls. Interested, he tugged at it, as the wearer must have done, but it wouldn't budge.

At that point he remembered his shaving razor and hastened back to his room, clutching Abigail's hairpiece. He sat on his bed, carefully cut away the tangled strands and examined the little comb.

It was designed as a simple cluster of

flowers—poppies, perhaps. In the centre of each nestled a clear, white stone—four in all. They looked like good ones, very, very good ones, and each by itself would have made a handsome solitaire ring.

Allington licked his lips. If they really were diamonds then the comb could be of great worth, considering the gold setting and possible antique value as well. It was definitely the work of a top-class craftsman and obviously not a modern piece, but his vague and patchy knowledge told him no more than that. He thought in terms of four or five thousand pounds, which turned out to be a rather timid estimate.

Ralph marvelled at the carelessness of a woman who could leave such a thing lying around in a wardrobe. And Colin—didn't he realize what it was worth? In fact, did he know it was there at all? Didn't anyone notice and wonder what Mrs Wylie had paid for it? His thoughts returned to the heaps of cheap glitter on Abbie's dressing table. To the casual eye it may have seemed like just another trinket, for it came from a more flamboyant age and was gaudy by Edwardian standards. He began to recall Barbara's complaints about her late sister and they appeared to confirm his theory.

'... irresponsible ... didn't comprehend the value of money ... took to spending as other people take to drink ...'

Overcome with excitement, Ralph slipped the comb into an inside pocket and turned head over heels backwards on his bed. After some moments he composed himself and, noticing that it was nearly twelve, scurried along to the Wylies' room to replace the false hair.

Later, when Barbara joined him for lunch, she fondly thought that his bouncing cheer was rapture from the previous night. Sad to say, Ralph had all but forgotten that.

THIRTEEN

Ralph had not dared to tell his wife that he was staying at Gypsy Hollow for the weekend. He simply disappeared for two days and it was only on Sunday evening that he paused to consider the trouble which awaited him when he got home. After his cosy and very profitable weekend with Barbara the thought of facing an enraged Primrose pleased him not at all. He wished he could extend the visit indefinitely but such was not possible, for Wylie would be back on Monday. There was, however, an alternative. Feeling somewhat drunk with success, he remembered that fortune generally favours the bold and therefore suggested to Barbara that they might take a short holiday together.

'Ever been to London?'

'Once or twice. I went last year, actually, just after my sister died.'

'What did you think of it?'

'Very exciting, but I was hardly in the mood to enjoy it properly. I had such a lot on my mind.'

'Quite, quite. That's understandable. But now that you've recovered from your loss, wouldn't you like to go again?'

'Certainly, but ...'

'With me?'

'Oh, I don't know about that ...' she began warily.

'Why not? I'm a man of substance. We could stay for a week—two weeks if you like. It's the least I can do after your splendid hospitality.'

'It's just a bit unexpected.'

'The best things usually are. I should know. I've always been impulsive and, um, unconventional.' He beamed at her and winked. 'Come on, be adventurous.'

Barbara dithered for an instant, wondering if there was any good reason why she should not go. The idea was certainly attractive.

'We can take the eleven-thirty train tomorrow,' pressed Ralph.

Barbara allowed herself a faint, malicious smirk as she mentally listed the gains to be made. What a shock for Colin when he got back! She did not want to hear an account of his weekend with Hilary—and how satisfying it would be to eclipse their little outing with a grand stay in London. It would do Colin good to know that she was not waiting around for his return. Oh yes, the advantages were too many to ignore.

'I know an excellent hotel where the food is superb,' continued Allington.

'What about the expense? I admire your generosity but I couldn't accept ...'

'Nonsense! I'm uncommonly lucky with money. Heaven provides, you might say.'

'I didn't know botanists were so well paid.'

'We're not. As it happens, I had a small

windfall recently. And, seeing that Primrose has chosen to desert me, I propose to share it with you. Besides, I have a spot of business to transact while we're there. If it is as profitable as I suspect then I shall take the opportunity of buying some property. Your presence would bring pleasure to a tedious commercial trip—and I may call upon your excellent taste and judgement when buying a house.'

This appeal to Barbara's conceit was the clinching factor.

'Very well, if I can really be of help.'

Allington's grin was wolfish. 'Barbara, you can't imagine how much you've done for me already. I think I can safely say that these two days with you have changed my life.'

'Heavens, you're exaggerating!'

'Not a bit. Shall we go and pack?'

Never before had Ralph failed to come home. For the first forty-eight hours Primrose was frantic with worry. She paced around; she peered anxiously down the road for some sign of him; she sat up all night, cursing and fretting, listening for his key in the lock.

Finally, exhausted, she made herself a cup of tea, ate some cheese and pickles with the remains of a stale loaf and resignedly went to bed at seven o'clock on Sunday evening. It was almost noon the following day when she awoke. Still no Ralph.

Now that the initial panic was over she began to consider the situation logically and came at last to a reasonable conclusion: either he had been arrested—in which case she would have been notified—or he had a woman somewhere.

How could he? After all her self-sacrifice, all her drudgery and scrimping. Primrose's sharp, dark eyes glittered with temper. If anything had happened to him the police would have informed her. Furthermore, Ralph was not the sort to go off on his own with no one to look after him. He was much too fond of home comfort for that. No, it had to be a woman—probably some fine and lofty piece with beautiful clothes. Primrose glanced down at her stained, woollen skirt, brown and shapeless. Her blouse, which had once been blue, was faded to a light, greyish colour, the shoulder seams twice mended. She had just one smart set of clothes, bought two years previously, and they had never been worn. She looked on them as precious and saved them for a special occasion—which, of course, never arrived.

A woman with plenty of money. No doubt Ralph would relieve her of some of that—but maybe she could afford it. Some female with plenty of time to be amusing, to listen to his silly stories and believe, as Primrose herself had done, that he was something of a tycoon. A woman who was, in every way, more entertaining than his own unpaid skivvy.

Bitterly she thought about the heaps of washing, the digging and planting, cooking and cleaning. She had polished his shoes for him, carried buckets of water to fill his bath by the fire. The list grew longer and the pictures in her head spread themselves out into a grim array of dreary chores. All her memories, all the years of her marriage amounted to nothing more than a catalogue of toil, discomfort and anxiety. And now, to crown it all, he was being unfaithful to her. He had also taken her savings.

'All men stray,' her mother had said, 'some more than others. We have to be patient.'

Primrose had no time for that sort of fatalism. Other men, who lived normal lives and provided security for their families, might be entitled to the odd indiscretion. Hers was not. His past sins were too many and she was not prepared to overlook this one.

Seething, she struggled into her old green coat and slapped on a small, round hat. Its flowers drooped mournfully over the stiff little brim as if in sympathy with the outraged face beneath.

Ralph had taken the gig with him on Friday afternoon, so she would have to walk the six miles into Jennyport. Stoutly, she set off, determined not to come back without him if he could only be caught. If she could just find the gig then the odds were fair that Ralph would not be far away. Had she known that he and Barbara were already halfway to London, Mrs Allington could have saved herself a long, weary walk.

It was not until five that evening that Primrose, footsore and miserable after her trek and a fruitless search around Jennyport, finally gave up and trudged home again. Thus, yet another item was added to the list of crimes she was compiling against her husband: blisters.

FOURTEEN

Ralph and Barbara arrived in London at four o'clock on Monday afternoon. He found a motor-cab outside the station and gave the driver the address of a hotel in Kensington.

It seemed to Barbara that the volume of traffic had increased dramatically within the past year, or perhaps she had simply been too concerned with her own affairs to notice such things on her last visit. Motor-buses and a few remaining horse-drawn trams rumbled and rattled around the bustling streets as London went about its business.

All her doubts and reservations about the trip began to evaporate. Admittedly, Ralph was not her first choice as a male companion but he was amusing and, equally important, he was going to foot the bill. Barbara made up her mind to enjoy her stay to the fullest—all the better to inflict the details on Colin and Hilary when she got home.

The Rushmill Hotel was sufficiently smart and expensive to impress even Barbara. She had, in the past, said of many hotels that they were less elegant than her own home. This one, however, was undeniably grand and promised two weeks of glorious cosseting.

Their room was spacious, decorated in soft shades of coral and cream. Its main feature was a bed which might comfortably have slept four and the easy chairs had the same plushy, welcoming look. The windows overlooked a public park, frothing with fresh greenery, with magnolia trees and Japanese cherry.

Barbara's eyes shone with approval and more than a little surprise. She hadn't expected anything quite so imposing. Slowly she took off her hat and tossed it on to a chair, delight written all over her face.

Ralph grinned as he watched her. He knew Barbara well enough to understand her snobbery and love of grandeur.

'Will this do, Madame? Is it acceptable?'

'It's lovely! I must say, you do have excellent taste.'

'I'm glad you're pleased. Let's see—it's just after five. I suggest we eat at seven-thirty and spend a quiet evening here to recover from the journey. I'll try and get my spot of business completed tomorrow. Hopefully, it won't take long and then we'll go out together in the evening. Agreed?'

'Yes, of course,' said Barbara blissfully. 'Anything you like. I'll leave all the arrangements to you. So far you've handled everything perfectly.'

The transaction which Ralph so urgently wanted to complete was, of course, the selling of Abigail's comb. Early next morning he set off from the Rushmill in a hansom cab to seek out an old acquaintance.

Nostalgia nearly swamped him when the cab drove away and left him standing in a shabby old street well-known to him from his younger days. For a moment, though, he couldn't spot the place he was looking for. There had been a great many changes.

The shop front had been altered. The brown paint which Ralph remembered was gone, replaced by white, and there was now a bay window in place of the old flat, square panes. The sign, however, still said *Dancey's Junk & Bric-a-brac*.

The goods, too, were just the same. Second-hand novelties, things dredged up from the cellars and attics of old houses. Scrapbooks and Victorian postcards, money boxes and model engines, ear trumpets, woodcuts, musical instruments and countless other items of interest to the specialized collector or those in search of mementoes.

Abel Dancey's establishment was best described as quaint. It was certainly not smart or expensive and gave no hint of his true prosperity. Indeed, there were few who realized that the old man had a fifteen-bedroomed country house in Sussex, surrounded by thirty acres of parkland.

Those few were Abel's real customers, the ones with whom he traded in 'special' articles. They were always close personal friends or people who came to him via the recommendation of such friends, for Abel was a cautious man. With Ralph he shared a dishonesty that formed the very fabric of his soul—but he was clever at it and that was the difference between them. Ralph had neither the intelligence nor the flair which had brought success to Abel Dancey.

'Ralph? Is it you?'

Allington chuckled. 'You've got a good memory, Abel.'

Beaming, the little bald man grasped him by the hand.

'For a moment there I wasn't sure. Must be over ten years—and you didn't have the moustache in those days. Wait a minute, I'll lock up and we'll go inside for a good old talk.'

He scuttled around the counter and slid the bolts on his shop door, top and bottom. Ralph followed him into the sitting room behind the shop, where Abel conducted much of his more lucrative business.

'How's that little dark bit you married? Can't recall her name now.'

'Primrose.'

'Ah, yes. That's it. Still together?'

'We're still married,' said Ralph evasively.

'Living in London?'

'Um, no, but I'm thinking about it.'

Abel took off his spectacles, polished them on his waistcoat and perched them back upon his nose.

'Is there some special reason for this visit, Ralph?'

Allington grinned. 'You can always smell

business, can't you, Abel?'

'I believe I can. Have you got something for me?'

From an inside pocket, Ralph produced the comb and placed it in front of the other man.

Dancey picked it up, turned it over, peered, squinted and frowned. Finally he stared at Ralph over the top of his spectacles.

'How the hell did you come by a thing like this?'

'I thought you'd be impressed.'

'Wait here.'

Abel got up and disappeared into a tiny back room in which were kept the tools and instruments of a jeweller and watchmaker, together with volumes of hallmarks and registration marks for precious items of every sort.

When he returned, Ralph was almost bouncing with expectation.

'Well, are you interested?'

Abel sat down and considered for a

while. 'French,' he said quietly, 'eighteenth century. Probably saw some good times before the revolution. I'll give you eight thousand—guineas, that is.'

Allington nearly choked. 'That much?'

Abel gave a faint, snorting laugh. 'Good God, you had no idea, did you? What were you expecting?'

'Four or five thousand, perhaps.'

Dancey laughed again and said with a trace of irony, 'You're lucky I'm an honourable thief, Ralph. I could have fleeced you on this transaction and you'd never have known the difference.'

Allington blushed slightly.

'But the offer stands. Eight thousand. To tell the truth, the comb is worth more like eleven thousand—but that's my profit. I don't do business just to break even. Do you want to think about it?'

'When can I have the money?'

Abel handed back the comb. 'Call again this afternoon.'

Ralph decided he could go farther and

fare much worse. Abel Dancey could always be relied upon for discretion.

'All right. Two o'clock?'

'Three. And Ralph,' the older man said softly, 'if you've got any more of these trinkets, you know where to come.'

'I only wish I had.'

Later that day, Ralph made his first big purchase—an Austin Seven, brand new. It was the latest model, not a large car, but neat and nippy. He felt it suited his personality.

'Good grief!' said Barbara when he took her out in it that evening. 'Your business deal must have gone extremely well.'

'It did,' chuckled Ralph, patting her knee. 'Barbara, dear, you've brought me luck.'

'You poor child!' boomed Cora Millston-Blight. 'The worthless wretch! Cuthbert, she ordered, 'give her a brandy.'

Her husband, a patient, willowy old man of sixty-three, moved in a permanent aura of mild resignation. No one knew if he had always been so or if it was a matter of natural adaptation in response to the forceful personality of his wife.

She was one of those robust country ladies with little time for genteel nonsense. She was also something of a crusader with a genuine, if heavy-handed, desire to aid the afflicted. There was something exhausting about Cora—hence, perhaps, Cuthbert's gentle languor. He made no attempt to keep pace with her, but acted instead as a counter-balance. It seemed to work, for their marriage chugged along quite smoothly.

'How long has he been gone?'

'Four days,' said Primrose glumly.

'You have no idea where he is? And not even a letter?'

'Nothing.'

'You're quite sure he hasn't come to any harm?'

'Seems unlikely. I would have heard by now.'

Cuthbert handed her the brandy.

'Thank you. No, it's a woman, all right. He's been spending a lot of time in Jennyport lately and always goes out wearing his best clothes.'

'Then I think you're well rid of him, my dear,' said Cora stoutly. 'Only a worm would do such a thing to a good, loyal wife. Isn't that so, Cuthbert?'

'Yes, dear,' he said automatically.

'Abominable behaviour.'

'Loathsome,' agreed Cuthbert absently, seating himself before the fire and wishing Cora would leave him alone.

'How are you placed for cash? Can you manage without him?'

Primrose snorted. 'He didn't contribute much anyway, so that's no loss. But I did have fourteen pounds saved up. I kept it in a pickle bottle behind the flour barrels. Ralph took it all. I didn't think he knew it was there.'

'Hmm. Should have kept it about your person, my dear. Sew it into your corset next time. Not to worry, though. That's easily remedied. Cuthbert, your wallet, Please.'

'Oh, no,' protested Primrose. 'Please, I don't want ...'

'Let's have no arguments. It's a matter of necessity.'

'But I can manage.'

'No doubt you can. I'm not attacking your independence, Primrose. The money is merely a loan to help you through a crisis. The fact of his desertion is burden enough without the added weight of cash shortage. You can repay me as and when it's convenient.'

Her husband produced his wallet and handed it over. Primrose, embarrassed, shifted awkwardly in her chair as Mrs Millston-Blight took out twenty-five pounds. Cora meant well, as always. The loan was made with no trace of condescension. All the same, Primrose was reluctant and glanced uncomfortably at the old man. His sly wink and smile said, Take it. It'll make her happy.

'Thank you. You're very kind.'

'Practical, dear, just practical. Did you say he took the gig with him? In that case you must borrow one of ours. You'll need it when fetching supplies.'

'I don't often go into town. I'm almost self-sufficient.'

'Nevertheless you must have the gig, then you won't feel stranded. Yours is such a lonely house. Do you ever feel nervous at night?'

'No. I'm not the timid sort.'

'Quite right. Splendid. And remember, my dear, whatever problems arise you can always bring them to me. Rejoice in the fact that you'll have less work to do without a husband to look after.'

'True,' said Primrose thoughtfully.

'Men can be very ageing, you know. They have a way of sapping one's energy.'

Cuthbert looked quite pained at that. No

one could accuse him of sapping Cora's energy. Quite the reverse.

'Pamper yourself,' she went on. 'Have the odd lie-in, buy some new clothes. In the end you may not want him back at all.'

Primrose secretly allowed that life might indeed be easier without Ralph, but she had no intention of letting his defection go unpunished.

The first week of Barbara's holiday was such a success that she almost forgot Colin in the excitement.

They visited exhibitions at Earl's Court and the Alexandra Palace, art galleries and museums, Madame Tussaud's, Hyde Park and the London Hippodrome. The entertainments seemed virtually endless.

Ralph, being a native Londoner, knew exactly where to go, and each morning after breakfast he would whisk her off to some new place of interest. They lunched every day in a different restaurant, always the best, always with champagne.

After a while, lost in the euphoria, Barbara ceased to wonder when the money would run out, nor did she care how much he lost at cards. In fact she encouraged him, for gaming fascinated her and as she had no intention of marrying him he was quite welcome to bankrupt himself.

One evening as they came out of the Lyric Theatre, where they had been to see 'The Chocolate Soldier', Ralph said, 'I thought I might look at some houses tomorrow. Would you like to come with me or would you rather go shopping?'

'Shopping, I think. You don't mind, do you? I'm sure you don't really need my help when your own taste is so obviously faultless.'

'Fine, fine. You go and enjoy yourself.' He fished in his pocket and gave her thirty-five pounds. 'Later on we'll go and see "The Quaker Girl" at the Adelphi. Would you like that?'

'Oh, Ralph! You really are the most

generous man I've ever met.'

So it was that Ralph Allington went off alone next morning in search of a large and stylish property—something to compare with Gypsy Hollow. Barbara's home had impressed him greatly and he quite fancied himself as the owner of a similar establishment.

It was late in the afternoon when he found the one he wanted. If anything, it was more impressive than Gypsy Hollow—a beautiful four-storeyed town house in a fashionable district. A house with a portico, chandeliers in the hallways—and electricity, too. The owners were already considering a generous offer from another buyer. Without a second thought, Ralph topped it by five hundred pounds and the matter was settled by six-thirty.

He was weary when he got back to the Rushmill and found Barbara somewhat peevishly waiting for him, dressed ready for the theatre.

'Wherever have you been? You didn't

tell me you'd be so late. We'll have to hurry now or we'll miss the start of the play.'

He flopped down into a chair and eased off his shoes.

'Look, um, if you don't mind I'd rather not go. Not this evening. Tomorrow, perhaps.'

'Yes, I do mind, countered Barbara. 'You promised and I've spent two hours getting ready.'

'I'm tired, Barbara. I've looked over seven houses today. My feet are sore and I've not had supper yet. Just for once I would like to stay in.'

'This is most inconsiderate of you.'

'I found a house. Aren't you interested?'

'Not in the least.'

'No?' Allington's brown eyes twinkled with an odd sort of amusement, which annoyed her. He seemed to be savouring some private joke and she felt somehow disadvantaged.

'Wouldn't you like to see what I've

bought?' (With your money, he added inwardly.)

'I couldn't care less.'

She got up and pulled impatiently at the buttons of her coat. One of them flew off and rolled under the bed. She flung off the coat and dropped it on the floor.

'What are we supposed to do this evening? It's only a quarter to eight.'

Ralph shrugged. 'Have an early night?' he suggested pleasantly.

'Why? You've done nothing to deserve it.'

'Dear me!' He clasped his hands comfortably across his stomach and stared up at her in mock dismay. 'I didn't realize that bed was a matter for bargaining. Was I wrong to think you enjoyed it?'

Barbara floundered at that. The implications were most insulting and she had been careless to invite such a remark.

'I didn't mean it to sound like that.'

'Of course not. Now, I'll have a light supper sent up with a bottle of champagne.

How does that sound?'

Her response was a watery smile as she began to undress. She had looked forward to seeing 'The Quaker Girl' and an evening of indifferent sex with Ralph seemed like a poor substitute. Just for once she would let it pass, accept this disappointment as a small flaw in an otherwise perfect holiday. All the same, he had better not make a habit of it.

That incident was perhaps the first rumble of approaching strife. Thereafter it subsided for a while and not until ten days later did the real trouble begin.

FIFTEEN

The longer Ralph stayed in London, the more reluctant he became to return home and face his wife. Now that he had made his escape it would be sheer lunacy to go back and surrender to a vengeful Primrose, who would never again let him out of her sight. Nor would she consent to move to London and live in his new house. No, indeed. She would probably make him sell it.

It would be so simple to disappear in a vast city like London. The odds were good that she would never find him. With hindsight, it seemed fortunate that Barbara had declined to look over his town house. She did not even know the address and so could not convey that information to his wife. How tempting, how seductively easy to vanish into the bustling life of London, his beloved home town.

If he was honest with himself—and even that was something of an effort—he would admit that the intention to stay was born from the moment he stepped off the train. Now, after almost three weeks, Barbara was talking about going home and Ralph consciously made the decision that he would not be going with her. He elected not to mention this until the last possible moment. Barbara might change her mind, offer to stay on with him and, sad to say, Ralph didn't want that. She was a demanding woman in terms of both money and attention. Ralph didn't like being fettered and he had no desire to exchange one nagging female for another. He wanted freedom.

No, Barbara had been a diverting companion but enough was enough. She would, in the nicest possible way, be packed off home with memories to treasure of a glittering holiday and never a suspicion that he had robbed her of over eleven thousand pounds. That, at least, was the theory. The actual course of events was to prove rather less smooth for him.

Some remnant of conscience assured him that it would be churlish, indeed cruel, to simply abandon Primrose without a word of explanation. She might worry about him, he thought fondly. And she had, after all, given him twelve years of faithful, if irritable, domestic service. They had even shared a few good days and it was this that prompted him to send her a farewell letter, plus a box of chocolates with which to console herself.

He was careful to give no indication of his whereabouts and it seemed, when he dropped the parcel in the post box, that his marriage was henceforth ended.

So it might have been if Barbara had not sent a picture postcard to Colin on the very same day; just a brief note to assure him she was enjoying herself and thus, with any luck, fuel his jealousy. With glee she imagined him casting Hilary off in searing temper and boarding the first train to London, whereupon he would storm into the hotel to drag Barbara home where she belonged. To this end, it naturally was necessary to state the address of the Rushmill, plus room number, boldly upon the card. This she did, without the faintest notion that someone else might be far more interested in that address than he was.

Primrose sat forlornly upon the tattered sofa in the parlour. At her feet lay a heap of crumpled brown wrapping paper. On her lap was a large box of cheap chocolates with a picture of a gaiety girl on the lid.

Primrose looked exactly as she felt—tired and defeated. For the moment there was neither shock nor anger—those would come later—just a dull, flat acceptance that he would not be coming back. In the weeks of his absence she had faced the possibility and assured herself that he was no great loss, that life would be much improved without him and that she could gladly shrug him off like the burden he was.

Reality, however, proved surprisingly brutal. This postal dismissal seemed so impersonal, so insulting. She read the note again. It was brief and full of fumbling, smarmy clichés. Her face was expressionless except for a wry twist at the corner of her mouth as she sifted out the predictable old phrases.

'Please forgive me ... better this way ... sure you'll understand ... new start for both of us ... get over it in time ...'

There was nothing here of special relevance to Ralph and Primrose who had lived together since eighteen ninety-eight. Anyone could have written those words. He had probably dredged them up from some book or play.

Primrose screwed up the note, then jumped slightly as the hollow rapping of the front door knocker sounded through the house. She tossed the chocolates aside and went to answer it.

'How are you, dear? Bearing up? I've been out giving Calibar his walk and thought I'd call to see you.'

Cora's great bulk filled the doorway and beside her on the step squatted a rather doleful bulldog.

'It's very nice of you. Please come in.'

She led the way into her parlour and indicated the best armchair. 'Have a seat.'

Cora subsided into the chair and the dog slumped across her feet.

'I'll make you some tea.'

'No, dear, no. Jolly kind but I had a late breakfast this morning.'

'Oh,' said Primrose absently, 'I see.'

'Is something wrong? You seem a bit preoccupied. And what's all this?' Cora pointed to the wrapping paper.

'I've had a letter from Ralph—and those.' Primrose nodded toward the chocolate box.

'Ah! Gift of appeasement, eh?'

'No. Just a parting shot.'

'Whatever do you mean?'

'He's not coming back.' Primrose searched

around, found the little ball of paper and handed it to her employer.

'Thoughtless animal!' declared Cora. 'Do you suppose he means it?'

'Looks pretty final to me—and he wouldn't dare do it as a joke. Besides, the parcel was postmarked London. He always wanted to go back. Now that he's actually done it I don't suppose anything could drag him away.'

Cora was still scanning the note. 'Hmm. No address, I see. Who's this Barbara he mentions? Someone local?'

Not for an instant did Primrose recall her brief meeting with the woman who had bought some eggs on that long-forgotten day in nineteen hundred and six, and the name certainly meant nothing to her.

'I don't know,' she said wearily. 'Just some woman he's met.'

'And now he proposes to abandon you without any further contact. I would call it a blessing, my dear, if it wasn't for one small problem.'

'What's that?'

'Well, he hasn't actually divorced you, Primrose—or given you the opportunity to legally rid yourself of him. As things stand, you can't remarry for quite some time, can you?'

Still reeling from the blow of desertion and with only twelve years of shattering conflict to show for her marriage, Primrose was hardly amenable to the idea of a second try.

'That doesn't bother me in the least. I shall never marry again.'

'Nonsense, dear! How old are you?'

'Twenty-nine. Nearly thirty.'

'Gracious. Marvellous age. The thirties are wonderful years, Primrose, I assure you. I enjoyed mine immensely. Extreme youth can be very painful, dear. Trial by fire, you might say. Most of life's booby-traps seem to spring on one in the early years when one is ill-equipped to deal with them.'

Primrose smiled weakly.

'Of course you're upset now. That's to be expected. But it'll wear off and you'll be all the wiser when you come to choose another man. I admit they're a bit trying at times but I wouldn't be without Cuthbert, you know. He's a dear old boot really. Now, as I understand it, you'll have to wait something over two years. After that the divorce should be a matter of formality. Desertion with adultery, you see. Quite straightforward. And you must keep this.'

She flourished Ralph's note.

'It's not much but it may be useful in court.'

Primrose was developing a headache as Cora chattered on in her loud and hearty voice. By way of interruption she picked up the chocolate box and offered it to Mrs Millston-Blight.

'I'm afraid they're not very good quality, but would you like one?'

'Never say no.' Cora selected a chocolate and bit into it. 'Hmm. See what you mean. Too sugary. Never mind. Calibar!'

The bulldog opened one eye and peered up at her. Cora dropped the chocolate in front of him. He ate it mournfully and settled down again, only to grunt in annoyance as she jerked at his lead.

'Don't get too comfortable. Time we were off.'

She lumbered to her feet and turned to Mrs Allington.

'Brace up, dear. Don't lose any sleep over him. And remember—I am your ally. You can always count on my support.'

'I'm sure I can.'

Primrose showed her out and watched her striding up the road with Calibar's bow-legged figure trotting along behind.

Cora's brusque reaction had somehow dispelled the initial shock. No, it was not a tragedy and yes, she would recover. But why should he get away with it? To dismiss her like a redundant servant—and with a cheap present, too. Indignation mingled with a scorching, helpless fury. If only she knew where he was, Primrose would see to it that he suffered for his treachery, besides which there was still the matter of her fourteen hard-earned pounds to be settled.

SIXTEEN

'Don't like cod,' grumbled Ivy. 'Don't like fish of any sort. Gives me the wind.'

'Then leave it.'

'What else have you got?'

'Not much. Bread and butter. Bit of cheese.'

'Is that all?' Ivy snorted. 'Fine thing when you visit your brother and he can't serve up a decent tea for you.'

Sammy snatched away the plate of cod and boiled potatoes.

'Your visits are getting to be a habit. God knows why. You do nothing but moan.'

'With a brother like you, I've got plenty to moan about. Tight-fisted, that's what you are.'

'Aggravating old devil,' muttered Sammy.

He went outside and dumped the

254

rejected food in the bin. His sister remained at the table, chewing moodily on a crust of bread and butter as she cast a critical eye around his cottage.

'You're a messy old sod, aren't you?' she said as he returned and dropped the plate into an enamel bowl already full of dirty dishes. 'Never seen so much old junk and wreckage lying around. No room to move.'

'I like it this way.'

'No doubt you do. Never had a wife to teach you any better. Why don't you get somebody in to clean the place up?'

'Are you volunteering?'

'Me?' squawked Ivy. 'You'll be lucky.'

'You reckon I should have a housemaid then, do you?'

'I wouldn't trust one of them,' said Ivy scornfully. 'Always creeping around, bowing and scraping. Half of them are light-fingered.'

'You wouldn't mind having one to look after you though, eh?' retorted Sammy, setting a cup of tea down in front of her and taking the seat opposite.

'Like Madam Abigail, you mean? And that snooty sister of hers?'

'Abbie was a good lass ...' began Sammy.

'I know, I know.' Ivy sounded guilty. 'She was never one for airs and graces, I'll give her that. And she didn't deserve what happened to her. But that other one she's vicious.'

Sammy chuckled. 'Barbara's a bit lofty and self-important, but ...'

'Vicious,' repeated Ivy. 'You men don't always see these things. You might notice a flash of spite now and again but you don't know how deep it goes. That Barbara—she hated Abigail. Hated her. How do I know? Maybe it's because I'm no angel myself. But I saw it. I recognized it.'

For a minute Sammy didn't speak. He ran a hand thoughtfully over his cheek and chin, digesting the idea, glancing dubiously at his sister.

'Yes,' she went on, slowly nodding to

emphasize her point, 'and I'd stake my very life that she's glad to see her dead.'

The old man stared at her, appalled. 'Ivy, you've no cause to say that. I know there was no love lost between them but the girl couldn't be that callous.'

'No? At first I thought she was just sore about the money. The day she came to see me 'twas clear she was smarting over the way old man Kendrick divided his will. But there's more to it than that. It's him, too. Abbie's man.'

'How the hell can you know that? Come on, Ivy, you're guessing.'

'All right, I'm guessing—but it's a good guess. She's taking a damned long time to get wed and I reckon it's him she's waiting for.' The old woman giggled with coarse delight. 'And 'tis easy to see why. He's a fine, toothsome bit of goods. If I was thirty years younger I'd queue up for a tumble with one like him.'

'You're a crude old devil, Ivy. 'Tis time you forgot about such things.'

Ivy cackled. 'Does no harm to think. Anyway, if you've got nothing else to eat I might as well go home and make a bit of stew. Don't know how you've managed to live on rotten old fish all your life. No wonder your back yard's full of stray cats ...'

She nattered on as he fetched her coat and hustled her out the door.

'I'll come again,' she said, planting a shapeless felt hat squarely on her head. 'You're not much fun but you're all the family I've got left.'

'Thank you,' said Sammy dryly, packing some tobacco into his pipe. ' 'Bye.'

Ivy didn't relish the idea of walking home. She had hoped that Sammy would offer the money to hire a cab but he said he didn't even have the price of a pint of ale. Considering his meagre stock of provisions, Ivy thought this was probably true. Their brief discussion of Colin, however, had given her an idea. Maybe that nice young man would be kind enough to take her home again, as he had done on regatta day.

She stopped at the gates of Gypsy Hollow and peered in at the mellow old house, half hidden by the shrubbery. Then she pulled back the iron latch and started up the path.

Heather grumbled and cursed as she hurried to answer the rapid, impatient knocking and was greatly annoyed to see Mrs Whickle on the step.

'Yes?'

'I've come to see Mr Wylie.' Ivy's tone was haughty and her face defiant as she recognized the woman who had so roughly ejected her from Abigail's reception.

'What for?' asked Heather, placing her large self firmly in Ivy's way.

'That's no business of yours. I'm family, if you remember.'

'He's got company,' said Heather, unmoved.

'I don't care. Tell him I'm here. That's your job, isn't it?'

Heather's broad features contracted into a scowl.

'It's part of my job to keep misfits of all descriptions out of Mr Wylie's house. So far as I know, you've had no invitation.'

'Hmph,' said Ivy, with vast contempt. 'Servants. Always running around after other people. Yes, sir, no, sir, grovel, grovel.'

'What I do is an honest job of work ...'

'Ladies, please.' Colin, hearing the squabble, had decided to intervene before things got out of hand. He winked amiably at the maid.

'It's all right, Heather. Thank you.'

She hustled off with a final backward glare at the old woman, whose face softened into a coy little smile.

'I was just passing and I thought I'd pay you a call.'

She casually patted her nest of stringy hair.

'You're on your way home, I take it?' He had guessed instantly what she wanted.

Ivy nodded hopefully.

'Well, in a while I shall be taking Miss Borlase home, so if you don't mind waiting ...'

'That's all right. That'll do fine,' she said eagerly, then, 'Miss who?'

'Please come in. I'll introduce you.'

Ivy swaggered into the drawing room to cast a curious and critical eye over the strange blonde woman sitting by the fireplace.

Hilary looked amused and faintly puzzled as he introduced them, aware that this pugnacious little character was making a stern assessment of her. To Hilary's relief, Ivy seemed to approve.

'Pleased to meet you, I'm sure. I like your dress,' she added generously. 'Suits your colouring.'

'Thank you. I got it in Paris.'

Ivy sat down on the settee, rather close to Colin, and her eyes widened. 'Paris, is it? Very posh.'

'I lived there for four years.'

Mrs Whickle seemed more and more impressed. 'I always wanted to travel,' she said sorrowfully. 'Mr Whickle never had the money though. I did go to Bournemouth once, for a week. Nice, it was.'

'Bournemouth is very pleasant,' agreed Hilary.

'Will you be staying over here now, or is it just a holiday?'

'Oh, I shall definitely be staying.'

'Can't see why anybody would want to leave Paris to live here,' sniffed Ivy. 'Dull I call it.'

'Well, there is a reason.' Hilary looked at Colin and winked. 'Shall we tell her?'

'Of course. Hilary and I will be getting married next year.'

'Oh!' Ivy stared from one to the other, cocking her head from side to side like a puzzled sparrow. 'No? Really?'

'Yes. Probably in the spring.'

'Well! Didn't expect that. Congratulations, I s'pose.'

The news came as quite a surprise but

she was not displeased, for the girl was likeable enough and a malicious delight began to expand in Ivy's mind as she realized what it would mean to Barbara Kendrick.

'When was this decided?'

'A few days ago. We've been thinking about it for quite some time.'

Ivy inclined her head with an evil smirk. 'Well, I must say I'm all in favour.' She leaned confidingly towards Hilary. 'I've always said he's much too good to waste. You see to it that you look after him properly.'

'Oh, I'll try.'

'You are hereby invited to the wedding,' said Wylie. 'And we promise not to imprison you in the attic, cellar or anywhere else.'

The old woman gurgled with glee. 'And what does lady Barbara have to say about all this? Bit of a shock, was it?'

'Barbara doesn't know yet. She's not here.'

'Oh,' said Ivy, crestfallen. 'Where is she?'

'In London on holiday—with a friend,' he added discreetly. Fishing in his pocket he produced a picture postcard and handed it to Mrs Whickle. 'Here. This came yesterday.'

The writing on the back meant nothing to her but she was quite taken with the illustration on the other side.

'Nice picture. Buckingham Palace, is it?'

'Yes.'

'Hmmph. Typical. I s'pose she'd like us to think she's been there for tea.'

'To be fair, Barbara hasn't mentioned any such visit—unless it slipped her mind. She seems to have been everywhere else though.'

'Snooty little madam. Still,' she said grudgingly, 'it is a nice picture. Do you want to keep it?'

Colin shook his head.

'Can I have it?'

'Of course. Now, if you're both ready, I'll take you home.'

Ivy tucked the postcard into a grubby pocket and got up.

'He's a good sort,' she assured Hilary when Wylie went to fetch her coat. 'He'll make a fine husband for you.'

'And do you think I'll make an adequate wife?'

'You'll do, dear, you'll do.' Ivy screwed her face into a gruesome wink and patted the girl on the arm. 'I approve. Anyway, I wouldn't have wanted him to marry that other one. God forbid.'

'You mean ...?'

'Yes, her,' said Ivy impatiently. 'Nasty, stiff-necked little cat.'

'Oh, she isn't that bad.'

'No? You wait. You'll find out when you tell her that you're going to marry him. She won't like it.'

'I'm sure I can deal with Barbara.'

' 'Tis to be hoped so,' said Ivy darkly.

When Colin deposited her back at the

cottage some time later, Ivy took the postcard from her pocket and propped it up against the clock on the mantel, high above the hearth. It was still there two days later when Primrose Allington made her customary call, bearing a basket of Ivy's favourite spring onions and two pots of home-made jam.

'How much do you want for them?'

'Sixpence,' said Primrose. 'Or fivepence if you've got a jug of milk to spare.'

Ivy thought that a fair bargain and she scuttled out into the pantry to fetch the milk.

'Fivepence, you said?' she asked, setting the jug down on the table. 'You'll have to wait while I go up and get it.'

Mrs Whickle kept her money tied up in a stocking which hung from a nail behind the wardrobe. It was all that remained of the hundred pounds that Abigail had given her and she guarded it like a dragon.

Primrose fidgeted irritably as she heard

the bumping and scraping sounds of the wardrobe being pushed aside. Silly old fool. Who would want to rob her? Even Ralph would be hard put to find anything worth stealing in this shabby old place ...

Her eye was suddenly drawn to a flash of colour above the fireplace. Men in uniforms, red tunics, polished boots. Buckingham Palace. London. She stretched up and took down the postcard, looking at the picture, knowing that Ralph was somewhere in that same city.

Who would write to Ivy Whickle from London? Especially as she couldn't read. The old woman made no secret of her illiteracy—in fact she was proud of it, with a defiant contempt for 'fancy stuff like that'.

Primrose flipped the card over and scanned the neatly written message on the back.

The name seemed to leap up at her. Ralph. For a moment it stood there in stark isolation, as if the other words had faded. Then she read on.

The card was from the woman, Barbara, and it was addressed to someone named Wylie. Who he might be and how Ivy Whickle had come by the postcard did not interest Primrose in the least, but the message itself set her shaking with indignation.

Ralph, it appeared, had been spending a fortune on this woman. Where he had obtained such funds Primrose didn't dare imagine, but her mind fastened grimly on to the knowledge that this Barbara person was being feted with dancing and champagne while she, his wife, had merited no more than a shoddy box of chocolates.

And there, at the top of the card, as bold as you please, was the address: *Room 307, Rushmill Hotel, Kensington.*

Primrose stared intently at it, committing it to memory. Then, hastily, she slipped the card back upon the mantel as she heard Ivy coming downstairs.

'Fourpence, was it?'

'Fivepence,' said Primrose stoutly.

Ivy sighed and handed her the coins.

'Thank you. I hope you'll enjoy the onions.'

Primrose was out of the door and treading briskly down the road before Ivy had time to answer. The old woman watched the thin little figure and observed with some puzzlement that Mrs Allington seemed to be in an uncommon hurry.

SEVENTEEN

Primrose had no intention of confronting Ralph and his woman in the shabbiness of her working clothes. She had already suffered enough humiliation without presenting the appearance of a household drudge for Barbara's amusement.

She went upstairs and changed into her best outfit, so long preserved in mothballs and tissue paper. The special occasion had finally come. It took some time to pin up her hair, for she had lost the habit of fashionable styling, but at last she achieved an effect that was quite elegant.

The finished product was a fresh and almost glossy Primrose. White lace, crisp and airy, foamed between the lapels of her burgundy top coat and relieved the sombre formality of a charcoal-coloured skirt. On her feet were shiny black button boots. A hat which matched the skirt was slanted so that its broad brim dipped slightly over one eye.

Staring into the mirror, she saw there a long-lost, almost forgotten person. There she was, Primrose Fuller of twelve years past, scarcely the same woman as the dowdy Mrs Allington. It was still a young face—which surprised and intrigued her, for Primrose had not felt young in a very long time. The drudgery had not marred her features in the way it had coarsened her hands. It had left instead a peculiar brand of dignity, a sort of world-weary assurance that said she could weather the worst in life. But, yes, still young. Cora was right after all. Perhaps there were good years to come.

And now? Yes, now she would catch the afternoon train to London. Her purpose was not to drag Ralph home again. Indeed, as Cora had predicted, she was beginning to feel happier without him. But he was not going to get away unscarred either. She had a few harsh truths to tell him, a few sharp words to leave him with a last, smarting memory of her. She would ensure that this foolish Barbara woman knew exactly what kind of worm be was. This time Primrose was going to have the last word.

Thankfully it was Wednesday—not one of her cleaning days, so Cora wouldn't miss her. The kitchen clock said ten to twelve. Plenty of time to take the gig into Jennyport and ... Ah, but no. She could hardly leave Mrs Millston-Blight's gig at the station if she meant to be away overnight. Best, perhaps, to go by way of Wellanford. It was only a small place but it was served by a halt station on the main line to London. The distance was a matter of two miles and Primrose could walk there in under an hour. She had not been to Wellanford for many years and it would make a pleasant change.

It was five-past twelve when Primrose

locked up the house and set off. She arrived at one and found the place quite lively with early season visitors. Due to this annual invasion, Wellanford had grown. There were several new shops and a rather smart restaurant had opened in the high street. Primrose had two hours to spare before her train arrived. She hovered for a moment, reading the menu that hung in the window.

Lunch in a restaurant. A meal cooked by someone else. This was a rare novelty. Eagerly she went inside.

Some time later, as she waited for the three o'clock train in company with some twenty assorted travellers, Primrose promised herself that there would be more such outings. Every Saturday, perhaps. She could save a little out of the housekeeping for her weekly treat.

The train pulled in slightly ahead of time and she found a quiet compartment at the front end. Four hours to London. Four hours to prepare herself for a final battle with Ralph and his woman. Two to one, perhaps, but Primrose felt more than ready to deal with both of them.

'What did she look like?'

'Who?'

'Your sister.'

'Half-sister. She was very plain.'

'Plenty of personality though, eh?'

'That is questionable.'

'How very odd.'

'What is?' muttered Barbara impatiently. 'Why do you keep on about Abigail?'

Allington shrugged and drummed his fingers on the steering wheel. 'Just curiosity.' He parked the Austin Seven alongside the kerb in front of the Rushmill. 'You didn't like her much, did you?' he said, helping Barbara down.

Her delicate features twitched with annoyance and the dark eyebrows lowered in a scowl.

'We had nothing in common.'

She swept through the swing doors in

front of him and waited while he collected the key from the receptionist.

'Nothing?'

'Oh, don't be tiresome!'

The receptionist glanced up and met Barbara's baleful stare.

'What time would you like your tea in the morning, Mrs Allington?'

'Eight-thirty,' she replied irritably.

'Is that lemon tea?'

'Of course,' snapped Barbara. 'How many times do you have to be told?'

'I always check,' said the girl stiffly. 'Some of the residents like a change from time to time.'

'Such efficiency! Hoping for a large gratuity, are we?'

'Come on, Barbara,' murmured Ralph. 'Don't take it out on the girl.'

He linked his arm through hers but she flung him off.

'For God's sake, stop pawing me.'

She stalked down the corridor ahead of him and got into the lift. The girl behind the desk turned to the telephonist.

'Did you see that? What an awful woman.'

'Nasty piece of work,' agreed the other. 'Spoilt.'

'I'll say.'

Barbara was sulking by the window when Ralph went in.

'Just what is the matter with you today?'

'I've got a headache.'

'Oh, a headache. Why didn't I think of that? Came on quite suddenly, didn't it? Just as soon as I mentioned your sister.'

'Rubbish. Anyway, I don't see why you're so interested.'

He sat himself cross-legged on the bed and grinned at her.

'I find it strange that a good-looking young man like Wylie would choose the plain sister in preference to you—which you may, of course, take as a compliment.'

'He married her for money.'

'I assume, then, that she was older than you and so inherited a greater share ...?'

'I am the eldest. She cajoled my father into favouring her.'

'Dear me. What a villainous wench!'

'I don't wish to discuss this, Ralph. You have no right to pry into matters which only concern my family and me. I have never presumed to ask questions about your wife.'

'Now that the poor lady is dead,' continued Ralph, 'I think it amazing that Mr Wylie has not seized his opportunity and asked you to marry him.'

'You are deliberately trying to provoke me.' The grey stare was venomous but Ralph seemed undeterred.

'Could it be that he has reservations about you? I believe there is a certain blonde lady ...'

'Ralph!'

'... of whom he seems inordinately fond.'

'Damn you!'

'Yes.' He nodded with a kind of grim satisfaction. 'That's what it's all about. That's why you're here. A gesture of spite, eh? A little stratagem designed to whip Mr Wylie into line. The notion has been growing on my mind for some days now. I think it must be the way you tense up whenever his marriage is mentioned.' He sighed lightly. 'It seems I must accept the painful truth that your fondness for me is just an illusion. What a cruel blow to a man's pride.'

'You don't look so very wounded, Ralph. I know for a fact that you're not the sensitive type and I don't see that you have much cause to complain. I concede that you've spent a little money on me, but you did so of your own volition. And I, in return, have submitted to your mediocre lovemaking without protest, tedious though it was.'

The bantering grin vanished from his face. He could easily accept that she was not besotted with him, that she meant, in fact, to use him for her own ends. Ralph understood this devious and self-seeking mentality. He could even admire her for it. But such a disparaging verdict on his sexual efforts was a stinging assault on his self-esteem.

With a tight, vindictive smile, Barbara noted the impact of her words and moved in for a second attack. 'I'm bound to say that I was totally inexperienced before I met you, and therefore did not expect too much. But even so, I was disappointed.'

Her eyes glittered with enjoyment and she sat down in one of the chairs, still smiling at him. 'All the same, on balance I would say I've had the best end of the bargain.'

'Would you?' Ralph slowly uncrossed his legs and got up. 'Do you think your tactics will work? Personally, I doubt it. I suspect that Miss Borlase will beat you to it—if indeed you were ever in the running at all. From what little I've heard of her, she seems to have a lot in common with his first wife. A similarity of character, if not appearance. I believe Mr Wylie is a very consistent man. He is looking for another one like Abigail and seems to have found her.'

'That remains to be seen.'

'On the other hand, one could argue that you have at least enjoyed a lavish holiday at my expense—and so the experiment cannot be called a total failure,' continued Ralph, wandering up and down, his hands clasped behind him.

'Quite. I imagine you are somewhat out of pocket. I have always been intrigued at how easily a man can be induced to part with his money. It's one of the weaknesses of your sex, this foolish need to impress by spending. Advantageous though, for any woman who has the wit to squeeze you dry.'

Allington suddenly emitted a great roar of laughter, rocking back and forth on his heels. Annoyance and confusion spread across Barbara's face as she thought back through her words and found nothing that should amuse him.

For Ralph the temptation was just too

great. He had not intended to tell Barbara where the money came from, but these priceless remarks demanded it. They made a sitting target of her and he simply could not resist.

'What would you say if I told you this trip didn't cost me a penny?'

'Are you going to produce a rich aunt?' scoffed Barbara.

'Not exactly, but a female benefactor, all the same.'

'Your wife, perhaps?'

'Good God, no! Poor old Primrose hasn't even had a new dress in years.'

'No wonder she left you.'

'Well,' Ralph cocked his head to one side and grinned, 'that's not exactly true. As a matter of fact I left her—but I won't bother you with the details.'

'The plot thickens,' said Barbara, bored.

'But to get back to the question of money—your sister was an extravagant lady, was she not?'

'Extremely.'

'Quite. And it must have been difficult to keep track of everything she spent.'

'Impossible,' admitted Barbara sourly. 'Colin refused to supervise or stop her. She frittered away an enormous sum, much of which is still unaccounted for.'

'How much?'

'That is none of your business.'

'All right then, I'll guess. Somewhere in the region of eleven thousand?'

Barbara stared at him as a vague and awful unease took hold of her. She didn't like the look on his face—and how could he possibly have arrived at such an accurate figure?

'Eleven thousand guineas, actually,' he said softly. 'I sold it for eight thousand. Pity, but one has to take what one can get.'

As the colour drained from her face he noted how it faded down through sallow shades to a greyish white, not unlike stale candlewax. He was mildly surprised to see that Barbara could look quite ugly.

There was certainly no other description for the twisting, tightening features. The bleak eyes swept over him like a blast of frosty air.

'Colin was right about you.' Her voice was low and steady. 'He said you were trash. You're a damned thief.'

Ralph faced that one out with a jaunty grin. 'A withering verdict—but I think I can live with it. I have, after all, received weighty compensation and if Mr Wylie's opinions had been of any concern to me I would have turned tail long ago.'

'Naturally an abominable thing like you would have no conscience, no principles ...'

'None at all, so you needn't waste time on moral reproach. Wouldn't you be more interested in finding out what your sister did with all that money?'

Barbara said she would not, but her face betrayed her. The missing money was one of the great enigmas of her life. She had spent countless nights thinking and dreaming about it, searching for some new idea. Now came the knowledge that she had somehow overlooked the obvious. How else could Ralph have discovered it so easily—and by accident?

'Of course you would.' He took a cigar from his breast pocket, bit the end off and spat it into the grate. 'Now, where to begin?' He pondered on this as he lit the cigar.

'What was it?' snapped Barbara. 'I don't want an epic saga. I just want to know what it was and where you found it.'

'Fair enough. It was a comb.'

'What?'

'A comb. One of those hair ornaments that you women wear to parties and dances. Just a little bit of frivolity—except that this one was hand-worked in gold and set with several fine diamonds. So you see, it was not a completely irresponsible buy.'

'Where? For God's sake where was it? I looked in every conceivable hiding place.'

'At the back of her wardrobe, tangled

up in a bit of false hair. Careless woman, your sister.'

'Oh God,' said Barbara faintly, 'those hairpieces!'

'Not such a strange place to find a comb, although I must say it was negligent of her.'

'And absolutely typical,' muttered Barbara angrily. Sharply she jerked her head up and glared at him. 'How much is left?'

'In terms of cash, very little,' he said, amused. 'You have expensive taste, Barbara, and you have indulged it unsparingly during the past three weeks. I wonder, my love, would you have been so generous with the tips, so profligate in your shopping sprees; would you have approved this hotel or encouraged me to gamble so recklessly if you'd known it was your money we were spending? Note that I say "we", because you yourself have been far more extravagant than I, more wasteful. After all, my own purchases can be described as lasting investments—the car, the house—whereas yours amount simply to a pile of female trivia and a few bouts of indigestion. In all truth, Barbara, I can't see that you are any more sensible with money than your late sister—or does that only apply when you think you're spending someone else's cash?'

Barbara got up and she looked murderous.

'I want the deeds to that house. I also want the car and every other item of value that you have bought with my money. Otherwise I shall go straight to the police.'

Ralph smirked. 'I defy you to prove anything. The only reason you even know about the comb is that I chose to tell you. Neither you nor Mr Wylie has ever reported the theft of such an item. Can you identify it? Can you prove you ever owned such a thing? I shall say you're making it all up out of spite because I'm leaving you. Hell hath no fury and so on.'

'I'll find the dealer. He'll back me up.'

'That'll be difficult. The man is a friend of mine and, like me, he is—flexible—in his business affairs.'

The blood came surging back to her face in a wave of dizzying temper.

'You contemptible bastard!'

Her voice was an ugly screech in which no trace remained of education or breeding.

Ralph chuckled. 'Dear, dear. What were you saying about trash, just now? Seems to me it doesn't take much to make a foul-mouthed street harridan out of you.'

Her fingers curled into claws. With a swift and accurate stroke the nails ripped across his face, scouring narrow tracks through the skin. He yelped and flinched away, pressing a hand to the smarting scratches. Three furrows, darkening with blood, appeared across his cheek and the side of his nose.

'Vicious little ...' He grasped her wrist as she raised her hand for another strike.

Barbara drew her head back and, sensing that she was going to spit at him, Ralph spun her round by the scruff of the neck and dumped her, face-down, on the bed. It was one of his few virtues that he never hit a woman, no matter how much she asked for it, and his many bouts with Primrose had bred a certain expertise in dealing with such outbursts.

'Let me up! Damn you! Get your great ugly bulk off me.' She was screaming now, wallowing in her fury, and Ralph cast a worried glance at the door. 'Get off me! I hope you die! I hope you get every painful, disfiguring disease known to medical science.' She twisted and squirmed but he kept a firm grip on her.

'Barbara, shut up,' he hissed. 'This is ...'

'Scum!'

'This is a crowded hotel and I'll lay odds they can hear you right along the landing. You are making a repulsive spectacle of yourself with the whole third floor as an audience.'

'Too bloody bad,' shrieked Barbara and then, inspired with a new idea, she howled, 'Rape! For God's sake help me, I'm being molested.'

'Don't be bloody silly.' He clapped a hand over her mouth and she tried to bite him. 'Who's going to believe that when wc've been living here as a married couple for three weeks?'

A few minutes later there came a hesitant knock at the door. Barbara, in her frenzy, didn't hear it. Ralph sighed and, releasing her gingerly, went to see who was there.

He had just opened the door a fraction when she kicked him from behind. Raising her skirts, she delivered a sharp jab to the back of his knee and he stumbled slightly. The door swung back and there stood the hall porter with the receptionist and a small group of inquisitive residents.

A silence fell. Ralph sat down, rubbing his injured knee, and the eyes of the onlookers turned almost in unison upon Barbara Kendrick.

With her hairdo a wreck, her face a swollen, crimson blob and a trickle of sweat visible on each temple, she stood as though rooted, the skirts still bunched up in her hands. Even the most tolerant person would have to admit she looked like a lunatic.

The hall porter coughed importantly. 'Can we be of any help, sir, and, uh,' he turned uncertainly to Barbara and muttered, 'Madam?'

Madam, suddenly appalled at herself, fled into the bathroom and locked the door.

'My wife and I had a rather spirited argument,' said Ralph wearily. 'Please accept my apologies for the noise. I assure you there has been no damage to hotel property.' He turned to the receptionist. 'If you'll be good enough to make up the bill we'll leave in the morning.'

They all hovered for a moment, the guests shuffling and whispering.

To conceal his annoyance, Ralph said,

'I'm sure some tea would help to calm my wife—and I'll have a large brandy.'

The porter nodded and withdrew, closing the door behind him.

Ralph glared at the bathroom door and wished he had not told Barbara about her money. The joke had not been worth the aftermath. He should have enjoyed it privately instead of making an enemy out of a very volatile woman.

To Barbara, sobbing in the bathroom, this passing loss of dignity seemed, for the moment, worse than the theft of her money. She felt foolish on both counts, but public disgrace was always hardest to bear. She gnawed at her knuckles and imagined what those people must be saying about her.

And sure enough they were having a good deal to say, especially the receptionist, who sat with her friend at the switchboard and debated whether the woman in 307 was entirely sane.

EIGHTEEN

Sometime later, Barbara went out. Embarrassment made her shrink from using the main entrance where she would certainly encounter the porter and office staff. She left instead by way of the public bar.

It was a busy evening and the bar was already packed with noisy, jostling customers. She wove her way through the crowd, wrinkling her nose at the smoky atmosphere, and finally slipped out unnoticed. She had no particular errand or destination in mind, merely a wish to get away from Ralph and from the hotel, to take a walk in the spring air and regain some composure. Then, perhaps, when her mind was clear and her wits returned, she might contrive some means of getting her money back.

Passing a police station, she hovered for a moment and wondered if she might enlist their help. However, as Ralph had so gleefully pointed out, she had no real evidence that such a comb even existed and certainly nothing to prove ownership of it. When she got home she would search once more through the receipts in Abbie's bureau, but the hope was a faint one.

Moreover, to explain her holiday with Ralph would mean censure, humiliation. What if it got into the papers? Barbara cringed at the idea—and with Abbie's death still chafing at her conscience, contact with the law seemed unattractive. Mournfully she walked on.

It was barely fifteen minutes after she had left that Primrose got out of a motor cab and marched purposefully through the front door of the Rushmill. In her new clothes she looked quite affluent and the receptionist gave hardly a glance at her. Just another customer. The Rushmill had three hundred and ninety guests and was also busy with non-residents who came for meals, dances and conferences. The girl seldom remembered individuals unless, like Barbara, they gave her cause.

Primrose climbed the stairs to the third floor and went looking for room 307. On the way she passed only two old gentlemen and thought the place uncommonly quiet. She supposed that everyone was downstairs in the dining room—for the evening meal was in progress—and wondered if Ralph and Barbara were also having dinner. If so, they would find her waiting when they returned.

Finally she found 307 and rapped upon the door. Inside, Ralph thought that Barbara had returned early and forgotten her key. He was tempted not to answer, but that would only provoke another row. Grumbling, he flung open the door with a scowl which dissolved instantly slack-jawed bewilderment and more than a little alarm.

'Hello, Ralph.'

Warily he stepped back and Primrose marched inside, slamming the door behind her.

'For God's sake, close your mouth. You look like an idiot.'

'What are you doing ...? How did you ...?'

'That's not important. Where is she?'

'Who?' said Ralph weakly.

Removing her hat, Primrose turned contemptuous eyes on him and he winced.

'Gone out,' he muttered.

'Without you?'

'We had a quarrel.'

'Hmph. So I see.'

Ralph fingered the scratches on his cheek and said nothing.

'Pity,' continued Primrose. 'I suppose you don't know when she'll be back?'

He shook his head.

'Well, I'm disappointed. I wanted to have a look at the creature who enticed you to abandon your wife. Is she beautiful or simply rich? Is she charming, amusing, clever, or just some poor vulnerable moron who swallowed all your financial fairytales?'

'You're looking very smart, dear.' An ingratiating grin appeared on his face. 'Very attractive. Just like a girl of seventeen.'

'Don't try and sidetrack me,' she snapped. 'If I'd come in my old clothes—the rubbish I've had to wear throughout my married life—I'd never have got into a place like this. They'd have thrown me out before I got ten yards. My God, just look at this place! I could slave for a month and still not afford one night here. Where did the money come from, Ralph? From her? Or did you steal somebody's savings like you stole mine? A charity fraud, perhaps?' The words, staccato clear, stung like a volley of hailstones.

'I won it at cards.'

'Liar. You never won a hand of cards in your life. Even I can beat you and I'm no expert.'

'Primrose, never mind where I got it.

We're safe, honestly. There won't be any trouble. You needn't worry. There's nothing she can do and now that we're together again I'll make it all up to you. A house—you'll have a lovely house. And a car, too ...'

Hands on hips, Primrose tapped her foot with mounting temper and her black eyes fixed dangerously on him as he stumbled through a veritable stew of promises and apologies. At last he faltered and fell silent.

'So, you robbed her, did you?' she said. 'And you want me to condone it, share in it. Does she know?'

'Yes, but as I said, there's nothing she can do.'

'Poor silly bitch! I'm surprised she didn't kill you, Ralph. I could have done so myself after you took my savings.'

He fidgeted uncomfortably.

'How much did you take from her?'

He stalled for a while. 'Um, a few thousand, I suppose. But I did it for you, dear.'

'Really? And what about the farewell note, my sweet? The fresh start and all the other queasy excuses.'

'I didn't mean it,' protested Ralph lamely. 'Barbara wanted me to write it. I did it to keep her happy. You know how it is. She even told me what to say ...'

Primrose, mouth pursed, was shaking her head in wry disbelief, so he shrugged helplessly and was silent once again.

'Do you know what really annoyed me, Ralph?' She began pacing to and fro, her skirts flicking and swishing as she turned, her eyes never leaving his face. 'Those chocolates. That battered box of inferior confectionery which you thought good enough for poor old Primrose. An adequate token of dismissal, eh? Nothing too expensive, beggars can't be choosers.'

Thus far, their argument had followed its customary pattern, the tried and true Allington fight formula: a tirade from Primrose followed by excuses, lies and repentance from Ralph. It was now reaching the stage where he knew she could not be pacified and he therefore felt driven to hit back. Her last remark was the turning point.

Putting his hands in his pockets, he said brightly, 'Oh, I wouldn't call you a beggar, Primrose. On the whole, faithful servants are considered one step above beggars. I'm sure a box of sweeties would be ample reward for the average housemaid. Perhaps you expect too much, my love. Getting ideas above our station, are we? Hmm?'

She stopped pacing, injury and disbelief written upon her face.

'What's the matter?' he went on. 'I am simply endorsing your own opinions. You've been bemoaning your skivvy status ever since we were married and I am finally agreeing with you. What a contrary woman you are! Don't you care for honesty after all?'

He wandered across to the window and stood there, watching the traffic go by.

'You see, Primrose, a man has to be practical. Servants, like old clothes, get worn out and have to be replaced from time to time. There may be a few years' wear left in you, but I was never a man to ride an old horse too hard. And of course there is an element of boredom involved ...'

He was playacting and enjoying every second of it—like a small boy teasing a short-tempered cat just to make it spit and watch its hackles rise. And like many people who love to annoy and provoke, he was wont to show the greatest surprise should the victim turn around and bite him.

Cheerfully he moved on to greater heights and new outrages. As his wife's hand closed upon the handle of a heavy crystal water jug, he was saying, 'In view of my new-found wealth I shall require smartly uniformed staff to reflect my financial status. Let's face it, Prim old dear, up until now you've always been a bit of a scruff and one new outfit won't make a lady out of you.'

Primrose raised the jug and swung it in a broad arc. In that fraction of a second before it fell, she realized that she might kill him—but it was too late for a change of heart. The weight and momentum of the descending jug made it impossible to check or divert the blow and it landed with a soggy crunch just above Ralph's left ear.

He didn't cry out. He didn't even grunt. He just buckled and toppled sideways to the floor and flopped slowly over on to his back. Dead. Quite dead. His eyes were wide open and the palms of his hands turned outwards in an attitude of surprise and reproach that said, 'Primrose! I was only joking!'

The side of his head was a dark, sticky ruin of blood and hair. It looked squelchy and Primrose began to feel ill. The jug, still held limply in her hand, hung by her side and a red smear crept sluggishly down, tracing the chunky, cut-crystal pattern.

'Ralph?' It was scarcely more than a whisper. 'Ralph! Ralph, get up!'

A spark of hysteria urged her to kick him and tell him to stop fooling around, but he was obviously beyond such measures.

Primrose sagged a little, for her legs felt shaky. Pressing a hand to her mouth, she let the jug drop. Several minutes passed before she pulled herself together and turned to the tray of bottles and decanters on the table. Numbly she poured a hefty shot of brandy and swallowed it straight down.

'I've killed my husband. I've murdered Ralph.'

She mouthed the words but they had no impact. At first there was a kind of merciful pause wherein the deed seemed quite unreal. By the time Primrose had recovered enough to really accept what had happened, the brandy had done its work and a grim, purposeful calm settled upon her. Later she might agonize over him, but for the present self-preservation took priority.

Primrose had never meant to kill Ralph and it was therefore unthinkable that she should be hanged or imprisoned for it. Oh dear, no. It was his own fault for provoking her—but sadly the law didn't make allowances for the tension and aggravation between a husband and wife. Primrose thought it very much to her credit that she hadn't killed him years ago.

The urgent thing was to get out before Barbara came back—which could be at any minute. Swiftly she pinned on her hat and picked up her purse, checking carefully to see that she had left nothing else behind. Satisfied, she opened the door very slightly and listened, praying that there would be no one in the corridor.

All was quiet. Encouraged, Primrose edged out into the passageway and closed the door behind her. As she hurried along, she noticed a few spots of blood on her gloves and hastily peeled them off, stuffing them into her pocket.

Twice she took the wrong turning and scurried in confusion around the corridors, but at last she came to the main staircase. At first floor level she encountered a group of young men and women, dressed for a night out in town. Thankfully, Primrose fell in close behind them. The office staff were busy booking in some late arrivals as she passed. The few yards to the front door seemed endless but finally she was outside and trotting down the steps, giddy with the mingling of relief and evening air.

Thank God! The words sounded gratefully in her head and she almost blurted them out loud.

Briskly she set off, anxious to remove herself from the vicinity of the Rushmill. About a mile down the road she hired a hansom to take her to the station. She had just missed a train and was obliged to wait fifty minutes for the next one. It meant that she would not get into Wellanford until two a.m. Resignedly, she went into the buffet and ordered a badly needed cup of tea.

At this point, Primrose remembered with sudden dismay the long walk from the station to her home. There would be no cabs for hire at two in the morning—but perhaps that was just as well. It was necessary to get back to Hallenhawke without being seen, even if this entailed a long, stumbling walk along unlit country roads.

In a moment of superstition she wondered if divine justice might arrange for her to be attacked by some lurking lunatic on the way. The road was lonely, even in the daytime, and a farm girl had once been assaulted ... But no. She pushed the idea aside. Retribution, if it came at all, would arrive in a police uniform. For tonight, the last hurdle would be Wellanford halt. Such a minor station might be unstaffed in the small hours and once out of Wellanford she could be home by three.

Sooner or later the police would come to

inform her of Ralph's death, perhaps with sympathy, certainly with questions. Getting safely home, thought Primrose dismally, was just the first step. Afterwards there would be weeks or months of enquiries to be endured, perpetual strain in hiding what she had done. And what if they accused someone else? Primrose groaned, realizing that she would have to own up if such a thing occurred. But it was no good to speculate or worry about that just yet. She would have to stay calm and take things as they came.

Beset with gloom, Primrose gulped down the remainder of her tea and drifted out onto the platform to await the southbound train.

Some twenty minutes after Mrs Allington had left, a chambermaid arrived at room 307 to turn down the bed. Her knock was unanswered and so she let herself in.

There followed a predictable uproar in which a crowd of onlookers, spurred by ghoulish curiosity, gathered outside 307.

A woman fainted skillfully into the arms of a handsome young man and was borne away with much clucking and concern. Theories and opinions were exchanged. Those fortunate enough to have been present at the earlier incident between Ralph and Barbara attracted great attention when they proclaimed that the murderer could be only one person. That woman.

'Violent,' they muttered.

'Obviously deranged,' they said.

'The poor man.'

'I've always felt uneasy in hotels. One never knows what sort of people one's neighbours are.'

The police were called. They listened to the comments and glanced at each other. They said, very fairly, that they would wait until Barbara was questioned before drawing any conclusions.

Gradually the crowd drifted away, until there remained only a small band of nuisances who hovered importantly around a rather annoyed police inspector.

At just after ten-thirty he was standing in the hall, talking quietly with the manager—and that was when Barbara returned.

NINETEEN

It seemed she had walked for ages through endless miles of streets. The evening sun had soon given way to dusk and then the sickly, haloed glow of the gas lamps. Silent rows of houses reared on either side of her. Sometimes, turning a corner, she would find a music hall, an opera house or a pub—momentary outbursts of colour and noise before she moved on to the next deserted street.

Absorbed in her own problems, she barely noticed that she was lost. Only when a nearby church clock chimed ten did she think about returning to the hotel. The idea of spending another night in that room with Ralph outraged her and she wondered if the Rushmill might have a single available.

There was just enough money in her purse for the cab fare back to Kensington and eventually she found a hansom for hire. Her feet were aching and although her temper had cooled she had found no way of getting back at Allington. Alone in the cab, she shed a few angry tears and assured herself that he wasn't fit to live.

The street outside the Rushmill was fairly busy when she arrived. Customers wandered or lurched from the public bar and farther down the road people were pouring out of a small theatre, climbing into cars, carriages and motorbuses. Barbara paid the driver and went wearily up the steps.

As the doors swung open before her there came an instant understanding that something odd was going on.

Three uniformed policemen stood in the hall and with them was a short, irritable-looking man in an overcoat, who appeared to be in charge. Behind them loitered a number of residents, some of whom she

310

remembered from earlier on.

She halted just inside the door. The theft of her money being uppermost in her mind, Barbara's first notion was that the police had come for Ralph. But how did they know? Who told them ...?

And then they saw her. One by one they turned to stare. Mouths popped open. There were mutterings and then a hefty, bejewelled woman elbowed her way forward to jab a quivering finger at Barbara.

'That's her! The one that did the murder!'

Her heart and stomach seemed to somersault. The words struck home, spearing their way straight to the old guilt that was always close to the surface. In logical response she thought of Abigail. For a second the accusing faces seemed to vanish and into their place clicked a brief image of her sister, dead at the foot of the stairs. The next impression was that of a noose and terror came flooding in.

'No, I ...'

'Oh, yes, you did, young woman. We know all about it. Everybody knows and the police have come for you.'

To those watching she looked a picture of furtive fear and desperation. Her eyes darted from one person to the next, questing for some excuse, a way out. The words that came were uncontrolled and therefore treacherous.

'I didn't mean to do it. I just lost my temper for an instant and it all happened so quickly ...'

'There!' piped the fat woman. 'See?'

Barbara ran. The doors swung crazily back and forth as she burst through them and bolted headlong down the street. Behind her there was shouting, scuffling and the heavy thudding tread of pursuers. Barbara knew that men could always outrun a woman when skirts and high-heeled boots served to slow her down. Already her breath was rasping under the pressure of her stays and waves of giddiness threatened an approaching blackout. Panic and confusion suggested that she might escape if only she could find somewhere to hide. Over there, perhaps? In the park?

Veering off the pavement, she dived across the road with never a thought for traffic.

It wasn't the car that killed her, for it was not travelling fast and the driver was quick with his brakes. But it struck her a glancing blow—sufficient to fling her backwards and right under the hooves of a horse-drawn vehicle coming the other way.

For Barbara there was a roaring and screaming and the yellow glare of approaching lights. Then came a dull thump as the breath was knocked out of her and suddenly she was rolling beneath the bellies of two frightened horses. Above her there was snorting, squealing, the clinking of the harness. Had she kept still, she would have been all right, but her awkward attempts to scramble clear just threw them into panic.

Hooves rained down in confusion as the animals tried to back up and step over her. Like Ralph, she died of a single blow to the head.

All around, cars drew to a halt and people came running from every direction. Across the road a woman was shrieking in fine, dramatic style and the car driver shrugged helplessly as onlookers clamoured to know what happened. Yet again, Barbara was the centre of attention.

Primrose was frightened. Confined in her compartment as within a gaol cell, she had nothing to do except ponder on what was to come. The darkness beyond the window was a screen and on it capered images of judge and jury while the rhythm of the wheels chanted out her sentence. Hang by the neck, hang by the neck, hang by the neck.

She was shaken from these broodings by the awareness that the train was slowing down. Nervously she got to her feet and lowered the window to lean out. Just five hundred yards up ahead was Wellanford halt. There was no one on the platform. The station was lit by a single gas lamp perched above the entrance gate but there was also a faint glow from the ticket office. Somebody was on duty. Primrose clenched her fists and cursed anxiously beneath her breath.

The train drew in and stopped with a jerk. Within the station house an elderly porter snorted through his whiskers as he wakened from a doze. Primrose got off and darted into a pool of shadow beside the parcels office as the old man shambled out on to the platform. He went up to the front end of the train and spoke to the guard.

'Somebody get off? Thought I heard a door close.'

'Couldn't say, Bert. Train's all but empty anyway. This one always is. Easy shift, eh?'

'No excuse for not doing your job,'

grumbled the old man. 'There was some-body ...'

The guard grunted and blew his whistle. Primrose glanced anxiously round her as the last carriage disappeared up the line. The only barrier between her and the road was a wooden fence. Primrose had climbed many a five-barred gate in her searches for mushrooms and it would be no hardship to hop over this little structure. She hitched up her skirts and clambered over the top as the old man's footsteps drew nearer. There was an unexpected drop of three feet on the other side and she landed with a crunch.

'Oi!'

Primrose took off like a hare, scooting up the road with her skirts flying.

Puffing, the porter leaned over the fence and squinted into the gloom but he could see nothing. He pulled off his cap and smacked it against the railings, blowing angrily through his moustache.

'Another bugger with no ticket.'

Muttering, he shuffled back to the office and fell asleep once more.

Primrose kept on at a hammering pace until she was out of Wellanford. She was obliged to slow down thereafter, for the country lanes were rough and pitted. Lack of care would mean a broken ankle.

She stopped and looked up, thankful for the half moon which allowed her a little light in moments when the clouds rolled back. There was a strong wind that night. Branches and bushes whipped and creaked on either side as she trudged on toward Maelan Carn. In years to come she would remember that walk under the mottled, grey-black sky as something indescribably eerie but not nearly as dreadful as the fears which travelled with her.

It was ten-past three when she got home and almost four when she flopped into bed, worn out with worrying. When sleep closed in it was dreamless and refreshing—which was fortunate. Tomorrow was going to be a difficult day and she would need a steady nerve. Had she but known it, Primrose was already close to safety, for the police believed they had found their culprit and no confession from Mrs Allington could be of any help to Barbara now.

TWENTY

Two hours after the police had left, Colin and his fiancée were still sitting in the drawing room at Gypsy Hollow, trying to digest the bad tidings. Stunned silence and disbelief had turned to dismay as the constable outlined the happenings of the previous evening. Wylie supplied such information as he could and the men went on their way, leaving two very bewildered people behind them.

'I suppose they'll have some sort of enquiry,' said Hilary vaguely. 'Is that what usually happens?'

'Damned if I know.'

'Felling a man with a water jug seems somehow out of character.'

'Unladylike,' he agreed.

'Exactly—and I can't quite believe that

Barbara would do such a thing.'

'Well, the police are satisfied she did.'

'Don't you think they could be mistaken?'

'Hilary, she virtually admitted to it.'

'I suppose so.'

'People are deceptive creatures—never quite what you believe them to be. Barbara always seemed very controlled and yet Abbie once told me that she had a fearful temper. All the same, I would never have guessed that she was capable of murdering a man. God knows what he did to provoke her. It must have been something pretty extreme.'

'I know and I can't help feeling sorry for her. Lord, what a waste of life! She was only twenty-six and getting run down in the street is a pretty undignified end.'

'On the contrary, I think she was lucky. They would probably have hanged her.'

Hilary shuddered. 'The whole business would seem less tragic if I thought she deserved it.'

'In one way she did. Barbara was rash and bloody-minded over Allington. I warned her to stay clear of him but she wouldn't be told. Of course I'm appalled at what's happened. I'm sorry for the loss of her life and for the disgrace that surrounds her. But you have to admit that she dug her own pit and fell right in.'

'Speaking of disgrace, I notice the tom-toms are beating already. The newspapers have got hold of it and tongues are wagging all over town.'

'Poor Barbara. She always hated scandal. I suppose there will be a concourse of morbid, curious gossips at the funeral. They'll wonder what the vicar can find to say about her under the circumstances.'

'It's bound to shock Allington's wife, too,' said Hilary. 'What a way to lose your husband.'

'They were already separated,' pointed out Colin.

'Nonetheless, I wonder how she's taking it.'

Primrose was taking it very carefully. She had prudently burnt her best clothes, much as it grieved her to do so, and gone to work as usual. She progressed mechanically through the morning's chores with mouth dry and stomach churning, but gave no outward signs of unease. She went home after lunch to await the knock at her door and, sure enough, it came while she was having tea.

They were kind. They were sympathetic. They were moved at the blanched and haggard face of this shabby little woman and the way her knees buckled when they announced that her husband had been murdered.

Primrose's distress was only too real. She did, indeed, feel dreadful, with the tight-throated chill and strain that comes of real fear. Luckily, it was taken for grief.

'The woman who did it ...' began the first officer.

Primrose felt as if she were falling off a cliff.

'... was killed shortly afterwards whilst trying to avoid arrest.'

Primrose stared at him.

'Street accident,' added the second. 'Died instantly.'

Aghast, Mrs Allington turned from one to the other.

'What?'

They nodded. 'We think she probably bolted after killing him and then had to return because she needed to collect some money. There were only a few coppers in her purse and they wouldn't have taken her far.'

It was frightful. Primrose didn't suffer too much regret over Ralph but this was the kind of hideous complication she had dreaded.

'Who was this woman?' she asked, miserably.

'A Miss Kendrick. Barbara Kendrick. It appears that she was Mr Allington's mistress. A well-bred woman, according to witnesses, but hot-tempered, possibly unbalanced. I believe there was an ugly incident earlier that evening, during which she kicked and scratched Mr Allington.'

'Anyway, she admitted to killing him,' said one.

'As good as,' qualified his colleague.

'She did what?' asked Primrose faintly.

'Caught off guard, you see. Just blurted it out. She may not have intended to kill him. The charge might have been manslaughter but it makes little difference now.'

Primrose was utterly confused and shook her head helplessly.

'Did you know the woman, Madam? She came from Jennyport.'

'Uh, well, I knew of her. Ralph left me, you see, almost a month ago. I knew there was someone called Barbara but I had never seen her. Um, there was a letter that he sent me.' She got up and searched for Ralph's note, then handed it to one of the men. 'It was the last I heard from him.'

'Hmm. No address, so he obviously didn't want you to contact him again. Tell me, did you know he had just bought a new house in London?'

'No.'

'I assure you, Mrs Allington, he had bought a fine, large house. I suppose you, as his widow, will have a claim to it.'

Primrose was thoughtful for a moment, then spoke cautiously.

'I think I ought to tell you that Ralph was not an honest man. A wife owes her husband certain loyalties and I would never have told you such a thing while he was alive, but Ralph has always been—devious, untrustworthy. To my knowledge, this place was all we had. It was the best we could ever afford. And if Ralph bought a fine, new house then I wouldn't like to guess where he got the money, because he certainly didn't earn it.'

Primrose knew all too well where that

money had come from. She felt guilty enough about Barbara Kendrick's demise and had no wish to add to the burden by profiting from it. Furthermore, it was wise, she thought, to be candid about Ralph's nefarious habits in case the police uncovered them anyway.

The two men glanced at each other.

'Ah.'

'I see.'

'Well, naturally we'll look into that. If anyone comes forward with proof of fraud or theft then that will obviously make a difference, but in the absence of any such claim the house may still become yours in the long run.'

'This may, of course, provide some indication as to why the woman killed him. She came from a fairly wealthy background and he might have swindled her in some way. Does that sound likely to you?'

'Oh, it's entirely possible,' said Primrose sadly. 'If not her then someone else, because I'm quite certain that Ralph had barely a penny to his name. We lived from hand to mouth from the day we were married.'

'We've already spoken to Miss Kendrick's brother-in-law. He was candid in saying that he didn't like or trust Mr Allington—but he made no accusations against him, either. He also gave us to understand that Mr Allington claimed to be a botanist.'

Primrose was genuinely amazed at that.

'Good God, no! He did a bit of weeding for Mrs Millston-Blight, that's all. Mind you, Ralph was always inclined to exaggerate.'

'Mrs who?'

'Millston-Blight. She employs me as a part-time domestic. She's normally in at this time of day if you'd like to have a word with her,' suggested Primrose, knowing she had a champion in the redoubtable Cora.

They said they would call there on

their way back to Jennyport and Primrose was much relieved when they got up to go.

'Will you be all right here alone, Mrs Allington?'

'Oh, yes,' Primrose smiled bravely. 'I'm used to it. And I expect Mrs Millston will be along as soon as she hears. She's always very kind.'

And sure enough, within the hour Cora flew to her aid with cups of tea and the usual common-sense attitude.

'Brace up, dear. After all, it's not your fault and he did ask for it.'

As Hilary had said, everyone in town was talking about Barbara Kendrick. The events in London were variously described as tragic, scandalous, mysterious—even exciting. Some of the older ladies were disgusted that Barbara had run off to London to engage in wild, fleshly pleasures with a married man. The notion conjured up erotic visions which made them feel quite faint. The fact that she had later killed him didn't seem to bother them so much.

Most of Barbara's young men were heart-broken or disillusioned. The faithful Geoffrey wrote a commemorative poem about her. It was printed in the newspaper and must have struck a chord amongst the romantics, for the 'Kendrick business' was gradually moulded into a sentimental love story so durable that it became local folklore. But the tale concerned only Ralph and Barbara. Nobody ever wondered about Abigail Wylie—except one. Only Ivy Whickle, when she heard the news, paused to reflect on that.

Alone in her kitchen, the old woman sat on the bench seat, staring into the fire. It was late afternoon and she was making a herbal decoction to ease the rheumatism that sometimes troubled her. Lulled by the gentle bubbling, she watched spirals of fragrant steam rising from the pot. And slowly, from a host of vague and disconnected thoughts, a question took shape.

So much for you, Madam. No more than a trollop after all, despite your fine clothes and posh talk. And 'twasn't enough that you stole poor Primrose's man—but you had to murder him into the bargain. And was he the first, I'm wondering? You'll be remembered for sending a man to hell before his time—but what about your sister, eh? What about Abigail? If 'twas in you to kill, then who's to say that Ralph was the only one? Still, that's something I can only guess at. And perhaps 'tis better that way. 'Twould upset Sammy all over again if he thought Abbie was pushed down them stairs. And there's no sense troubling Colin Wylie with things that are past. He'll have a new wife, come spring, and deserves to be easy in his mind, so I'll not mention it. I reckon lady Barbara fairly outsmarted herself in the end and that'll do well enough to satisfy me.

Ivy reached for the postcard and glanced at it one more time before tossing it on to the glowing turves of peat, where it curled and puffed into flame, leaving only a powder of ash.

POSTSCRIPT

I shall never understand why that stupid woman admitted to murdering Ralph when she knew perfectly well that she hadn't done any such thing. And if she had not flown into a panic she would have been alive today. I shall always have a certain guilt to bear—but I can hardly be held responsible for someone else's irrational behaviour. The more I think about it the less sympathy I feel for her. After all, she had no qualms about stealing my husband—such as he was.

Primrose stood in the hallway of Ralph's London house, thoughtfully tossing the keys in her hand. The deeds to the property, delivered some days earlier, were neatly folded and tucked inside her bag. Several months of checking had revealed no other claims for the house—for only Abel Dancey knew about the matter of Abigail's comb and he kept very quiet indeed. The legal processes were now complete and Primrose became the owner of number 12, Galen Terrace.

I don't think I want to live here. That would be too much like dancing on her grave. Anyway, whatever do I need with a grand house like this? I'll sell it and buy something smaller, put the rest of the money in the bank. Just fancy—I'm a rich widow. Never thought I'd see such a day but it's arrived and by God I'm going to make the best of it.

After a brief exploration Primrose stepped outside and locked the door behind her. As she walked down the road a fragment of Cora's hearty advice floated into her head.

'Never turn your back on good fortune, Primrose. The property is yours now and I'm quite sure you deserve every brick and beam of it. Life is very unkind to martyrs and shrinking violets, my dear. From now on, make sure that you're not one of them.'

Primrose had every intention of following that advice and, as she walked happily onwards, plans for the future were already forming in her head.